Book Ein
Prophecy of Love
Anna Pattison

BERKANO BOOKS

Dedicated

to The Lady, *Vanadis*

Contents

BOOKS IN THE NORSE PROPHECY SERIES

Book Ein – Prophecy of Love

Book Tveir – The Prophecy Unravels

Book Prir – Prophecy Transformed

This story was first published as *The Nordic Prophecy – Book Ein* in 2013. The 4th Edition has been expanded to prepare for successive books in the Norse Prophecy Series.

"When Freyja and Sven couple
and children are born
then we will trade with many
and our village will prosper."

Chapter One

Something woke her. Pulling on the sleeve of her dreams, something tried to get her attention.

The light poured through the window and splashed, white as the milk of her goats, across the uncovered girl. She had known it was to be a full moon tonight and the warm evening had called for leaving the heavy shutters open. A bright square of moon light was now upon her, cast from the window. Her muscular form, developed now as a young adult, was illuminated. Sturdy hips and generous breasts rounded out the white gown which encased her elegant frame like a cocoon. Her sleek, bare arms were sculpted by light and shadow. Strong capable hands were folded childlike under her cheek.

Her beauty, her strength, her tenacity, and even passion and innocence both, would have been well admired by her *amma*, her late grandmother. Had she been fully conscious, she would have heard a voice that could only be the spirit she had known for a short time in this life, living on. *Freyja, child, awake.* She fought to keep her eyes closed. She did not want to leave the land of dreams she was enjoying, but something woke her and a slight smile came slowly to her lips.

She stirred, catching her breath with an unconscious expectancy. A light breeze brought the summer scents. The faint salt, fish smell of the ocean below the nearby cliffs of the fjord reached her slightly flared nostrils. Colorful flowers and the growing garden next to the house sent their sweet fragrances. And of course, the farm aromas, warm and pungent. She was used to that mixture of smells. They could never disturb her. Besides, she always slept well and comfortably in the wooden bed carved in relief by the loving hands of her grandfather long ago as was the custom of Norse men. The knot work on the headboard made Freyja feel as comforted as her *afi* had and the dragon heads on both corners kept bad dreams away.

She forced her sleepy eyes open and glanced lazily around the room. Nothing seemed out of place or unusual. The walls surrounding her brought the woods indoors, their colors rich and warm.

Perhaps it was the night air. Her limbs prickled with tiny bumps, making the many little hairs on her flesh stand up. Curling her long legs up with a slight shiver, she realized she had thrown off her sleeping furs. The sheepskins were still under her making a snug nest so she pulled the furs up off the floor, firmly over her, and tuned her ears to listen.

Voices on the other side of the wall were a normal, near constant occurrence. The melodious female voice would belong to Arndis. The deeper male voice could be any one of the numbers of amorous men, from the nearby village or farms, who visited her mother. Tonight, she recognized that it belonged to, Ogmunder, the village Headman.

"You already owe me one chicken. I should always ask you to pay before. Where is my chicken? Last time you said you would bring a chicken," chided Arndis.

"Calm, woman. I will, I will. Helga counts them every day," replied Og evasively. "I will bring you one next time. Now, I must get back to my own farm and the day ahead."

"Well go, but you cannot stay again unless you bring something more than one drinking horn of mead. You owe me for many visits. Now get out. We will wake my daughter," Arndis spoke earnestly in a low voice as she pulled Og out her doorway.

"The girl will not be bothered. She is used to this. Perhaps it will stir her own juices," laughed Og as he grabbed Arndis roughly around the waist and pulled her close. He spoke heatedly into her neck, "You know I could bring more than one chicken if I could have that hearty flower. Perhaps a milk cow!"

"You know that that is not possible," Arndis hissed as she slapped his hands away, "Freyja has another future. She must fulfill the prophecy."

As she listened, Freyja breathed in deeply and her head cleared. She remembered what drove her to wake. She had a constant dream, both waking and sleeping. Again, she thought she heard a feminine whisper, *Freyja, inn matki munr.* She was suddenly filled with a desire to make her dream a reality. Her heart pounded and her breath quickened, making her bosom rise and fall in rhythm. She could picture him, more real than any dream. A beautiful vision, so clear she felt she could almost reach out and touch him. He was her desire. He would fulfill her future.

She quickly wrapped her old grey shawl around her shoulders and left her room in her light under gown. Walking through her doorway she turned and came face to face with Og and her mother standing in front of the skin drape to her mother's room. Og's large hairy arm was draped around Arndis's neck and across her chest. His fingers ran across the fabric of her gown tracing the outline of her breasts.

"Now, I will bring you a milk cow if only you would let me have her," grinned Og. "I would certainly pay more than twelve *ells* of cloth to have such." He reached out with greedy hands toward Freyja, but she skirted away then pushed open the heavy outer door.

"Where are you going at this time?" Arndis yelled after her. "You must watch what you do, you do not want the life of your mother. Besides..."

"You are for Sven," her mother and she both said in practiced unison.

Neither needed to finish the sentence since they all knew she, Freyja, was for Sven. It had been said by everyone for as long as she could remember, though it now seemed some, like Og, did not want to be reminded of the words of the foretelling.

Freyja's bare feet flew swiftly down the steps. They barely felt the cold wood. These steps had been worn almost smooth over several generations of use. Farmers, hunters, warriors; both men and women had trod them regularly.

Freyja ran to the make-shift corral attached to the barn. Here she deftly moved a bark covered log to free the old stallion from the other side. She grabbed his mane and pulled herself up in one well-practiced movement to straddle his wide back. From the corner of her eye, she could see her mother push tonight's customer out the door. With a shake of her head and a half smile, Arndis pulled the door closed. Just before it shut, she glanced up with a worried eye toward her daughter.

The horse plodded easily into the green undergrowth and trees. The dark thick trees of the forest soon parted to reveal a small meadow. A breath-taking pool of light, every grass blade glistening, welcomed them. The horse lowered his head with a whicker and his lips nimbly gathered the grasses heavy with dew.

Freyja sat tall on the back of the horse. Her shoulders proud and back held straight, she was every bit the image of the maiden of the *Vanir* for whom she was named. She imagined she was a shield-maiden and he was her war horse. She let slip the shawl that bound her strong shoulders then crossed her arms to grab and pull her linen under gown up and over her head. The white gown flew from her fingers and drifted like a cloud slowly to the ground. Her long honey-blonde hair shimmered down her back and across her shoulders. Her strong arms reached to the sky and every hair on them glittered, golden. Her back shone with facets like a polished stone in the moon light. She shook her fists at the heavens and then spread her fingers wide.

"*Odin,* hear me," she cried with all her might. "All my time I have heard I am for Sven. I am aching for *inn matki munr,* the mighty passion. I long to feel a man's touch, strong and warm, on my body. If I am for Sven, bring him to me." The ardor of her voice was equal to the vision she held of the man of her dreams. She pictured him from his head to his foot.

Sven was taller, by a head, though younger than she. He had always been beautiful. His golden curls caressed his well-muscled shoulders which led to the powerful arms that would soon hold her. His chest was strong and belly firm now that he was a man. His legs were well defined by the muscles that made him one of the swiftest of her people. Her breath came in quick gasps as she thought of him.

She fell back on the horse with a forceful exhale and was bathed in moonlight. The only item against her skin was the necklace given to her by her mother. She never removed it and it rested cooly against her chest. The breeze made the hair on her body stand up. She shivered, perhaps from that breeze or from the passion in her heart.

She spread her arms wide, opening her heart to the heavens, smiling. "This is for Sven," she whispered. Then she took some time to explore the wonders that would (hopefully soon) be shared with him. The fingers of both hands slid from the hollow of her neck to the valley between her breasts. "These should please Sven," she thought. Her hands continued down her womanly belly and then slid to the inside of her downy thighs. She imagined that the warmth she felt from the horse was from Sven's body and closed her eyes with a dreamy smile.

Remembering why she came, Freyja sat bolt upright. She jumped off the horse and ran to her own sacred spot. Her bare feet and body reveled in their freedom, a child of the woods and of the seasons.

At her sacred place, several large boulders created a natural grotto which she claimed as her altar. On the rock shelf, she kept several stones which she had roughly carved. One to be Sven and one to be Freyja. She pulled some long grasses intending to bind the two stones together. She felt a strange force push against each of her hands as she forced the two stones together, but managed to tie them securely. Her fingers tingled as she stood the bound stones upright on the altar. With an excited breath she knelt, placing one hand on the rich earth and the other toward the silvery sky.

"Hail the gods! I call on you to fulfill the prophecy that I am for Sven. I ask the twin brother and sister of fertility, *Freyr* and *Freyja*, to bring us together in love for the future. May your powers bind us together as this grass binds the stones." She made the sign of *Thor's* hammer, *Mjolnir,* as she had been taught and stood.

As she walked to the old horse she stopped and caught her breath with a new inspiration. She thought she heard the voice again, *Freyja is for Sven and Sven for Freyja, as foretold to us.* If she was for Sven, might the reciprocal also be true? Sven was for her? Somehow this idea thrilled her with a new sense of purpose and power. She could be the huntress. She no longer had to wait for Sven to come to her. With the help of the gods, she would capture Sven. She quickly turned back to the altar and laid the two stones down. The Freyja on top of the Sven.

With a purposeful hand she picked up her under gown and shawl. The fire within would keep her warm on her way home and though naked she felt no shame before the gods. Mounted on the old horse, she let him slowly pick his way back while she held the vision of herself and Sven together. She smiled as she imagined the warmth of their naked bodies intertwined. Then she knitted her brow with new concentration. How bold must she be to make this dream a reality? How would she take him and when and where?

Lost in such thoughts, she found herself at the edge of a pond. Her reflection stared up at her surrounded by the silver cliffs. The reflection waivered and shimmered and made her wonder. Would this girl be worthy of the promise? Would she be able to play her part to the advantage of her people? Was she up to the challenges that went along with the binding of her hair?

She did not have long to wonder. The sun's rays were peeking from behind the cliff and she would soon have much work waiting for her on the farm. The time for dreaming was over, but the vision remained in her heart. She would have to trust the gods to guide her in its fulfillment.

CHAPTER TWO

Several days later she found herself repeating her daily chores while still thinking about the visit to her altar. Feeding goats, milking goats, every morning. Then counting chickens and gathering eggs. Some nests were in the barn, but a few were like a treasure hunt, hidden about the farm. As a child she had laughed with joy at their clever spots. Today she hunted with an annoyed half smirk then found herself clutching two eggs together. She thought about the two stones bound together on the altar. Her heart ached to be as close to Sven as her stone was close to his stone.

She shook her head and looked around. These few animals she saw plus the old horse made theirs a poor farm. But then, they only had two mouths to feed. They subsisted on these animals, their garden, and Freyja's trapping. Anything extra was sold or bartered in the village. And of course, there was what her mother could earn. Food, drink, and sometimes trinkets were bartered for her valuable skills in passion. Perhaps it was a special customer who had given her mother the necklace Freyja now wore.

Arndis had presented the bronze coin to Freyja several years ago when the women of the village had held a ceremony for her coming of age. They thought it fitting that she should have a necklace as the goddess wore one. In truth, compared to the goddess' hers was very meager. It was also unusual, as it was only half of a coin, cut very roughly, with a hole drilled through.

On that night of the new moon, Arndis had placed it on a new leather thong and tied it around Freyja's neck. She had promised to tell her more about it at another time, in private. Freyja rubbed the coin between her fingers and had a thought to ask about it, soon.

Tending the *kalgardr*, or cabbage garden, was a constant chore and today was no different. The garden spanned the length of the house on the west side and she enjoyed the fact that it was under her window where she could watch the magic of growth. She hauled buckets of water from the well around the front and then pulled weeds. Tomorrow she would dig turnips and leeks and pick what cabbage and kale were ready to take to market. Besides selling what they could at market, she had other things to look forward to and she smiled in anticipation. Hopefully she would find Sven.

The "Old One" would be in the village as well, to share her stories of wisdom and perhaps cast the runes. Freyja felt drawn to the wise old woman and was always eager to learn more of her own fate, revealed long ago from this very source. The wrinkled face was set with piercing pale blue eyes. Freyja felt they could look deeply into her being and, at times, even look through her. As a child she had hidden from the old woman but was always retrieved from her hiding places, no matter how clever, and forced to go before her. The wizened lady always insisted on seeing both Freyja and Sven together. Once confronted with the old seer, Freyja became fascinated. Stories of past and future were recited in a sing-song voice, fueling Freyja's vivid imagination. Strangely, this was the person who made her feel most valued.

She hauled yet another bucket of water from the well and kicked a chicken on her way into the house. Some water went into the black kettle over the fire to which she added roots to start a soup. She would check her rabbit snares later to see if they would be able to add meat. The rest of the water would be used to wash her hair, even though it was not bathing day, for she hoped to see Sven in the village.

Standing near the fire, she undid one brooch of her apron over-dress and let the strap fall. She slipped her other arm out of the strap and let both sides fold down to her waist. She untied and pulled down the bodice of her undergown over her arms as well. Carefully, she laid the knife she always wore on the floor. Stripped from the waist up she knelt on the well-worn wooden floor. She bent her head, lifted her dark golden locks, then lowered them into the bucket of cool water, making what looked like a bucket full of swirling honey. She splashed the cold water on her neck which then made a playful stream as it ran between her breasts. The girl used a rag to scrub her neck and ears.

She wanted to be more than appealing when she saw Sven. Perhaps she would also wear some scented flowers in her hair.

She stood up to wring out her hair above the bucket. Two large and hairy hands grabbed her wet breasts from behind. They squeezed and tugged at her. "Ah, yes, this would certainly be worth a milk cow, instead of twelve *ells* of cloth," bellowed Og as Arndis pulled him off.

Freyja grabbed her knife from the floor and whirled about. Her cold wet hair whipped her face. "You are lucky for my mother, old man," she hissed. "Had she not pulled you off, there would be blood."

"And so spirited, too!" Og's voice faded as he was pulled behind the skin hanging over her mother's doorway. "Think about the milk cow."

Pulse pounding Panting and red-faced, Freyja dressed. She shivered as she pulled her wet underdress up and tied it. Putting her apron over the top brought a touch of warmth. She was not sure if she shivered with cold or anger. Her shoulders heaved as she carried the bucket outside thinking how much she would like to stop in her mother's room and pour it on Og instead of the garden. She returned the bucket to the well and noticed the same chicken that she had kicked. Og must have indeed honored his promise to bring a chicken. She debated momentarily with herself on adding it to the barnyard or the kettle. With a satisfied smirk she thought, "Well..., now there will be meat for the soup!"

Entering the house, she added wood to the fire and put another kettle of water on for dealing with the chicken. First, she wanted to go outside and comb out her wet hair. She would use the comb her mother had once been given. The comb was carved out of an unfamiliar beautiful substance from far away. When she turned it in the light it looked like the northern lights of the night sky or a rainbow. She held it now toward the sun and twisted it in delight. A childish pursuit, but it made her relax and brought a smile to her lips.

Outside, she sat on a rock in the sun and thought herself a siren, or perhaps one of *Aegir's* daughters, from the stories who sang sailors to their deaths. She would sing Og to a watery end on the rocky fjords as she combed out her golden locks. His hands had shocked and disturbed her, but they had also strangely aroused her. Her breasts had been made cold and tight by the water and had then suddenly been surrounded by warm, although rough, hands. The texture of the hands of another was a new sensation. None of the boys had even dared to be so near her. They all knew of the rune casting and were warned to keep their distance. They also knew the law codes, about premarital relations and the unintended consequences of a child. They could find themselves quickly married or at the very least supplying two-thirds of the support for such an offspring.

Being touched by another made her think of how she longed to be touched by Sven. Her eyes closed and she imagined his youthful arms wrapping around her from behind. Her own arms went around herself as she daydreamed. His embrace would be strong and warm, and he would love her. His eyes would smile at her then his mouth would caress hers. His touch would not shock her, but be tender and welcomed. Tomorrow she would make sure they would meet and perhaps soon, she would have him. She said yet another silent prayer to all the gods for their assistance.

She then turned her attention to the chicken and just a little bit of sweet revenge. She traded the comb in her hand for her knife and butchered the animal under her mother's window, making sure to make as much noise as possible. Her vicious plan was to continue the process in the same location and add some stench to the goings on inside.

The kettle of boiling water was brought outside so she could scald and pluck the chicken. Her arms ached as she held the kettle away from her body to walk down the steps. The movement was precarious, but worth the effort. Wet feathers soon flew into the window as she threw them wildly. She knew they would inconvenience her mother at the least. Poor Og, he would not get as much attention as he wanted.

Arndis quickly came to the window, "Child, why are you doing this here?" she growled.

"I must prepare the chicken Og so kindly brought to us," Freyja pretended to be innocent. "I was so excited to see it. We have waited so long and I was anxious to cook something tasty we could share with the important Headman who cares so well for you."

"Yes," boasted Og as he approached the window, scratching his naked, furry barrel chest. "I always bring you the best as is fitting of a Headman." He had not understood the sarcasm of Freyja's statement. Freyja choked on her laughter and quickly turned her head. Og was now fully framed by the window and was not clothed at all!

Freyja rolled her eyes as she went up the steps to add the chicken to the pot. Og angered her, but he had brought a chicken. He would never change and she would waste no more time thinking of him.

She lifted her chin, feeling that she had accomplished much this day. The farm animals had been cared for. The garden weeded. A chicken processed and cooked with a good root soup. Plus, her hair was washed, ready for Sven. Even Og could not ruin the promising vision she held for tomorrow.

She let her imagination run wild in front of the cooking fire. The vision was of Sven, tall, of golden hair. His strong limbs were rounded with muscles born of farm work and hunting. He was well spoken of for his running and climbing abilities. She had seen those muscles taut and glistening last summer when the boys were racing. She would know those limbs around her.

In comparison to those well-muscled limbs, his tunic lay smooth against his chest and hips. She would discover what lay beneath the tunic. She would have him and his passion. Surrounded by the kettles and herbs hanging to dry, she kept the vision strong and alive. The vision of love fulfilled.

Chapter Three

F reyja woke early and heard no voices. "Mother, all is quiet?" she whispered tentatively while knocking gently on her side of the wall.

"Yes, I am alone," Arndis replied with a yawn. Freyja smiled, delighted to find her mother unoccupied.

She went hurriedly about her chores and gathered together what they could to take to market. One basket was full of eggs and she had another brimming with fresh roots and new vegetables.

Freyja brought her mother some stew and sat on her bed while she ate. Arndis was in her thirties, the years just beginning to show. Her hair had darkened and then mixed with gray. She was a bit shorter than Freyja and of similar stocky stature, but with widened hips and tired, though ample breasts. Her dark blue eyes were surrounded by many laugh lines. Freyja always wondered how it was that her mother continued to be so positive though her life had been so difficult.

"Freyja, you look nice and you smell good. I hope you are not looking for a man at market," Arndis spoke with feigned surprise.

Freyja glanced down while she blushed. "Only for Sven," she answered.

"Good, I will keep the men off you and you will keep your legs closed. Eh?" her mother chuckled around a bite of stew. "I keep hoping for the prosperity foretold for us. Perhaps soon you will be ready to have your man and then be a mother. In the meantime, we get by and add to your dowry."

" Why do you wait for me to do this?" asked Freyja.

"You remember the story?" queried her mother. Arndis smiled knowing that Freyja had the story engrained in her heart and soul.

She did know the story, but she loved to hear it and it wasn't often that she and her mother were alone. Freyja shook her head, no, "Tell me the story, once more, please."

Arndis began, "The winter before you were two years of age there was much sickness. Many of the elders, including my mother, your grandmother, died." Freyja heard the familiar whisper, *Yes, many of us moved on to the other world to sit at Hel's table.* She shook her head to focus on her mother's words.

"The babies were also sick and all those who were younger than two years died."

"But, not me," interrupted Freyja.

"And not Sven," Arndis continued without a breath. "In the spring, the wrinkled Old One came into the village when we all were gathered for market. Someone asked her why there had been so much sickness and so much death of the very old and the very young. The Old One cast the runes.

She raised her staff high and spoke the prophecy. In her sing-song voice she said, 'the old always die to make room for the young. Our village is to go through changes to bring about the future. Our mothers were tested with the loss of their children, but more will come and one day there would even be prosperity for our village.' The Old One pointed at you and then Sven and then said, 'When Freyja and Sven couple and children are born then we will trade with many and our village will prosper.' So, you see why you must do this even though many others of the village have already forgotten," added Arndis.

"Like Og?" asked Freyja with a frown.

"Yes, the Headman and others now say that the Old One did not tell the future. They doubt her clear reading of the runes."

"I do not doubt and I will do this," shouted Freyja heroically as she jumped up and held her chin nobly high. She did not tell her mother how much she wanted to do this. She hoped to make the impression that she, Freyja, was ready to face her duty. "I will fulfill the prophecy."

She thought longingly of Sven. He had always been beautiful. Golden curls and a strong build. His sky-blue eyes vied with his bow mouth as his best feature. She wanted those eyes to look upon her with passion and wanted his mouth to meet hers in lust. She wanted him to write a *mansongar,* a maiden-song poem, for her. She already felt ensnared by her desire for him and did not fear the power of magic imbued in such a love poem. There were strange feelings in her breast and stomach when she thought of him, to be sure. She felt a tightness and a warmth in her chest. These feelings were new and intriguing to her, not fully understood, but seemingly not to be feared.

It was true that they had known each other all their lives, but they had not been too close. Sven kept only to his farm and family and the pack of boys who roamed the village lands together like wolf pups chasing each other through the woods. Freyja had been kept under watchful eyes, because of the Old One's prediction, and on their farm by necessity. Freyja and her mother had been fiercely hoarding her dowry for the day they all knew would come and she hoped for desperately. *It is now time. You are no longer a child.* The voice again. She felt comfort and encouragement surround her and now felt the voice was her grandmother's, soft and melodious. This guidance from her *amma* was a good omen and would be welcome.

While her mother readied herself for market, Freyja sat at the table absentmindedly tracing the wood grain of the ancient tree. A slow smile came to her lips as she thought of how she might accomplish the task she had put before herself. Sven was almost one year younger than she and had not yet even looked at girls with sidelong glances. He stayed on his own farm, as much as she, so they had little opportunity to see each other. She would vigilantly seek him out today and see to it that he noticed her. Then she would make Sven, the boy, into Sven, the man. She knew what pleasures she could give her own body and it seemed only natural that she would learn his body quickly. After that, it should only be a short time before the wedding negotiations would begin. She looked up when her mother's tapping foot brought her back to reality. Arndis stared down at her daughter with an amused look.

"I often wonder where you go in your daydreams, daughter. It is no matter," she shrugged. "It is time we were going."

The two women loaded their arms and began the long walk to the village. As they walked, they were joined by others. The twin girls from the next farm, fell into step with them. They liked Freyja, even idolized her somewhat. Last spring, they had helped Freyja put flowers in Og's hair when he fell into a drunken sleep, in front of the Mead House. He awoke when his plastered friend planted a kiss on the top of his balding head and the two got into a brawl that entertained everyone but the Headman. They retold the story when they passed by the Mead House and the owner, Hallig, waved to them.

By the time they had gathered at the meeting of three roads to tell stories and trade wares, the locals were in a gregarious mood. Laughter rang loudly and friends called out in greeting. Fresh early crops and the talents of the people were spread on blankets and benches. There was a beautiful white wool shawl made by the mother of the twins that Freyja could see herself wearing for Sven. She had nothing worthy of trade and consoled herself muttering, "You cannot eat wool." She was, however, ecstatic to trade the last of her roots for a wheel of cheese. A lucky family had milk cows, but not enough roots.

Down the south-east road a bit Freyja saw Sven with his mother. They were each carrying a large bundle. Her heart leapt at the sight of the young man to be her lover and her feet moved her forward without thought. Sven and his mother put down their bundles at the side of the road and his mother quickly began displaying their wares. "So many have already gathered. I told you we would be late. You men do not understand that women like to see all that is offered. Some may have left already." She went on muttering under her breath as she spread out a cowhide to place her whey pickled vegetables and *nalebinding* mittens upon. She was a local expert in the one needle weaving. "Open your bundle, Sven, and help me. I see traders coming."

Sven's mother was kneeling with her back to Freyja. Sven was standing to pass items to his mother and noticed the young woman. Their eyes met and he blushed. He straightened to brush off his clothing which emphasized his beautiful shoulders. For a long moment they could not take their eyes from each other. Sven ran his tongue over his teeth which made his lips look full and inviting. They both breathed deeply. Sven's mother reached out her hand to take something from him and there was no response. She looked up with a scowl at her son who stood frozen. Sven swallowed hard and stammered something to his mother then fled.

Sven's mother stood and turned around, her eyes watching her son depart with her mouth open. She slowly shook her head then saw Freyja. Both hands went quickly to her hips and her lips pursed. Her chin went up as she looked down her nose. "Do you have something to trade, girl?" she asked brusquely.

Freyja pretended to be interested in some mittens. "Not yet, but I am looking for later," she replied. She kept looking down, but felt the woman's eyes upon her. "Thank you," Freyja hurriedly whispered. She looked up to see Sven's mother standing with her arms folded, as a guard over her wares. "Your work is beautiful," she added hoping to sooth whatever animosity was there. Freyja turned to hurry back to her own mother. She was left feeling confused and uneasy. Did the woman not understand their connection? Did she not honor the prophecy?

She felt relieved to find her mother right where she had left her and Arndis's welcoming smile soothed her. Her mother had successfully traded many of her trinkets and made plans for a "visitor", a dark and handsome stranger. His long black hair was in braids wrapped with colored threads and decorated with beads of color, also. His fingers held several silver rings and he wore two layers of tunics of fine cloth belted with a fabric tie. He was tall and strong as his well-muscled calves advertised. He wore fine boots embroidered with designs and offered Freyja a shiny coin, unlike any she had ever seen, for the wheel of cheese she had just acquired.

"What is it? What do you think is its worth?" asked Freyja.

"It is a coin from very far away that men use for trade. Do you see the drawing of their sounds, here?" he showed her both sides. It shone silver, like a full moon.

"It is no good to me unless we can eat it," laughed Freyja.

"Perhaps," he continued, "you might wear it as you do the penny around your neck." He pointed to her chest.

Freyja grabbed the leather thong around her neck and found that the bauble on the end had slipped out of her blouse. "I only need this one," she stammered grabbing it.

"But look," he reached out to touch the coin. "Yours is just half of a coin with a rough edge. My coin is smooth, shiny and round plus it is without a hole," he persisted. Freyja pursed her lips and shook her head while tucking the necklace back into her blouse. "And as for its worth we could test it at the Mead House."

Arndis slipped her arms around him. "I will show you the Mead House and if you want the cheese so much you must come to our home. The cheese will be shared and more," she rubbed seductively against him.

"Cheese and both of you?" he bellowed with happy surprise. He looked back and forth between the two women.

"No," they snapped together as Arndis led him away toward the Mead House.

Freyja let out a sigh and fingered the keepsake around her neck. It was, as the stranger said, only half of a coin with a hole in it on a leather strip. Somehow, she had known it was only a penny, but she had not liked being told so. It must be special or her mother would not have given it to her at her ceremony. Had it come from another traveler to faraway places as all pennies and coins? She decided she would insist that her mother tell her the tale of the coin. It would fill a void, answer her questions. The stranger's comments made her realize that she needed to know about it and how it had come to her.

Something about the day seemed odd and she realized that she had not yet seen the Old One. She left the meeting of the three roads and walked toward the Mead House to see the object of her wonderings in the middle of a group. The Old One usually seemed to hold people spellbound, but something was wrong. The children were not sitting, listening quietly and politely, and giving the usual gifts of gratitude on which, she survived. They were dancing round the white-haired woman as she sat on a boulder, mimicking her. Freyja gasped when she realized that they were reflecting the mood of the adults.

"Where is our prosperity, old woman? We tire of waiting and our children go hungry," a rough woman taunted her.

"The runes have told us," the Old One began with a tired voice. "When Freyja and..." she stopped in mid-sentence when she saw the girl and straightened her shoulders.

"Yes, here is our goddess now," another woman grabbed Freyja by one arm and patted her belly. "I can see she is not round with child and Sven doesn't even know what to do with his manhood. We have waited more than sixteen summers. It seems we cannot rely on this idiot couple to plan their *Frigga's-day* wedding or your old worn out casting. You must cast the runes anew to see how we can make our fortunes better," she demanded of the old woman. The old woman began to tremble as the group around her became as agitated as the two outspoken women. Her ancient hand clasped her staff tightly as she grimaced.

"Patience people," Freyja knelt in front of the Old One. "We have survived much and for long, but the Old One has told us of our future and we must only be patient," she said a bit too enthusiastically.

"You, of course, would defend her. The prophecy is all about you, but you are too selfish to make it come true," bitterly spat a burly woman.

Freyja put her arms around the Old One and stood her up gently.

"I, for one," an angry woman said, "have patience which is wearing as thin as my body. I will find guidance somewhere else." She took her offering of bread with her. The group pulled back, muttering and began to disperse, most taking back their gifts as well.

Freyja walked the Old One, who was visibly shaking, to join her extended family, including Karle, at their market spot. They watched out for her and often brought her to the village on market days. "She is upset, some women were screaming at her. They now doubt her powers as seeress," Freyja explained. She could not look the old woman in the eyes and felt her face flush. *When Freyja and Sven couple...* "I still believe," she whispered and pressed the wheel of cheese into the Old One's bony hands.

Freyja kept her eyes down and turned to walk away when she felt the claw of the old woman's hand grab her wrist. The Old One pulled her backwards with surprising strength and whispered fiercely over Freyja's shoulder into her ear.

"You will also love of foreign born of Loki's tongue. Of raven hair and lips soft as a flower's petal. Of the blood of your family's clan." The Old One pushed her forcefully forward so that she almost stumbled.

The encounter with the angry mob had unnerved Freyja and now this? What was she to make of the Old One's words? She questioned the prophecy and herself under her breath as she approached the Mead House to meet her mother. What if…? She stopped the questions before they were asked. *Find Sven*, she seemed to hear.

It took a moment for her eyes to adjust to the room so much darker than outside. The flickering light from the fire and many candles felt soothing. Her shoulders relaxed. Soon Freyja saw her mother sitting on a bench between the stranger and Og at one of the several long tables. The laughter and smiles lifted her mood and the corners of her mouth. "Freyja, come and join us," yelled Og. He lowered his voice. "She is ripe for the picking, I keep saying, but they will not listen," he practically drooled as he leaned across Arndis to speak to the man. "I have even promised a milk cow for the honor of being her first." Og leaned back to grab Freyja, pulling her down on the bench next to him.

"Off, old man," said Freyja through clenched teeth, swatting his hands away.

"Now Og, tell me more tales of you and your friend here," Arndis grabbed his hands to put them around her. "Freyja, these men met many years ago elsewhere and just now Tahir has found his way to our village. I will enjoy their stories and entertain them while you go find your young friends."

"Thank you," mouthed Freyja as she stood to leave.

She saw Sven and caught her breath. He was so near, a walk across the room would bring her hands to touch him. Her hands tingled in anticipation of touching the body that she had never seen with her eyes. She longed for him to know her body as she did. What wonders would she know? What pleasures would they share?

Sven was surrounded by young men who would soon set out on a "viking". Each spring men from their village and the farms around would sail off. They would take supplies and hope to also find hunting or fishing to sustain them. If they landed near a settlement they might trade or raid for food, plunder, or slaves. Some had even returned with wives to start their own family, but their population was growing and farm land was becoming scarcer. Maps were created from these expeditions in hopes that some might return with their families to claim and settle new lands.

It would be Sven's first time and Freyja knew he would not return with a wife as they were promised. She smiled with satisfaction at this thought. Her ears rang with the stories of the men. They were loudly boasting, drinking, and laughing. It might be hard to get Sven's attention. Freyja lifted her chin and took a step.

She walked over, stood behind Sven, and boldly put her hands on his shoulders. They were firm beneath her fingers. He looked over his shoulder and then shrugged off her hands. A strong arm reached out and pulled her down. She found herself in the lap of an older boy, Karle, who pushed his face into her breasts. "This is what you do with your woman, Sven," he laughed and moved her to Sven's lap. Freyja threw an arm around Sven's shoulders and quickly kissed his face. He wiped off the kiss and reached for his mead, but he did not push her off. A smile blossomed on Freyja's lips.

She kept close to his body and savored the warmth and the strength he exuded. Her side pressed against his chest and his lap felt delicious under her. There was talk of the upcoming summer of raiding and wagers that Sven would be as adept as his father before him. Karle reached over more than once to pat Sven on the back. He smiled, winked, and pointed his chin at Freyja in encouragement. Sven seemed oblivious to the woman on his lap and was intently drinking up the praise of his lineage as well as the mead being bought for him.

"We will make a man of you Sven. Raiding and whoring," said Karle loudly. "Unless Freyja does it first," he looked pointedly into Freyja's eyes and slipped his hand up her skirt. She had been taking sips of Sven's mead and felt emboldened by it as well as her premeditated plan to conquer him. She was on pins and needles waiting for her opportunity and the touch to her skin only made those sensations heighten. She wriggled and grabbed Karle's hand roughly to remove it from her thigh, then almost choked on the mead as Karle licked his fingers. Karle stood and purposely raised his tunic to flash his genitals at Freyja in parting. Still, Sven seemed focused on his mead and took no notice as an amused Freyja watched Karle leave.

Freyja's eye was caught by some scuffling near the door. Og's wife, Helga, was dragging him out of the Mead House by his ear yelling, "I count one less chicken in my flock." She was saying something about a missing chicken and giving Arndis the evil eye.

A few moments later Arndis waved goodbye to Freyja with the handsome stranger in tow. She knew that meant that she would have to make her way home alone. It was fine as the path was well known to her she had always been safe from unwanted advances. Anyway, she was planning to be the one making advances tonight and hoped that she would be late in going home. Many people began to leave, staggering out alone or in pairs. Singing or romancing, wrapped in each other's arms. A fine ending to a fine day.

Sven soon noticed that the others had left and stood up abruptly, knocking Freyja onto the table. He mumbled something and stumbled for the door. Freyja followed; a bit wobbly on her feet as well. Her pulse quickened with her objective in mind. She tried to imagine what the goddess she was named for would do in this situation.

Outside, the moonlight made it easy to find their way and Sven's way was directly to a bush to relieve himself. As he finished, he wobbled backwards and fell onto a grassy mound. Without a second thought, Freyja flung herself next to him. She found her hand beneath his tunic and reached for his *kokkr*. Sven was quick to respond and Freyja positioned herself on top, her knees straddling him. She yearned to know his passion.

Her thighs tingled with the warmth of his skin. She reached her hands beneath his tunic to feel his belly then slid them up his chest moving the fabric up as well. The smooth muscles under her hands were a wonder. As she slid her hands upward her face came near his chest and she could not help but kiss his skin. Her lips reveled in the sensation of his nipples growing hard. Her chest lay against him, and another sensation was felt between her legs as she pressed against his hot firm flesh. She felt an urgency and sat up quickly.

She spread her legs wide, and her hand hurriedly searched for his manhood. She almost swooned with the thought that this act would fulfill the prophecy as well as leave her virginity behind. She would know a new phase of womanhood. She clumsily pressed her body down to meet his and was amazed at how well they fit together. They were making love! Her passionate response was a quickened heartbeat and breath. Sven began to moan and rock forcefully under her and in mere moments his tension was released in a warm flow. His movement stopped so Freyja stopped as well, but she was surprised how quickly it had gone. She wondered if there could be more.

"Sven, you are for me," Freyja spoke low as she kissed his downy cheek and rolled to lay beside him. She rested her head upon his shoulder and wrapped her arm around him. They lay still, their closeness creating an energy between them. She smiled, with all the possibilities now about to unfold. "We are beginning our future." He did not respond, but she snuggled closer to him. "The first of the prophecy is done." Still there was no response and she frowned. She raised herself up on one elbow to see that he was sleeping soundly. He had passed out.

She knew that this moment would start their representatives, *fastnandis*, to begin negotiations for their marriage. Their lives would be forever changed. However, this was nothing like the vision she had about their first meeting of love. Freyja had thought that something magical might happen. She would be filled with some new inner knowing, perhaps her skin might glow with warmth and pleasure. She had believed that at least there would be passionate wrestling and stifled groans and ultimately great pleasure for both of them. Both of them!

She stood angrily and glowered back over her shoulder at Sven's sprawled body. His snores were blatantly audible. She reached down to pull a clump of grass and threw it at him. Dirt exploded at his side and still he did not respond. Her lips trembled as she gathered herself together, found her bundles next to the Mead House, and began the journey home, alone. Her slow pace gave her time to reflect on this new phase of her relationship with Sven. If he did not remember tonight, it would mean nothing. If he did remember, then what? Would they fulfill the old woman's prophecy? Her lips pursed with a new fear and her eyes filled. No one had ever said anything about them being happy. Nothing was ever mentioned about her being fulfilled. No one had ever mentioned *inn matki munr*, the mighty passion, for them.

Chapter Four

M orning came with a new voice on the other side of the wall. It belonged to the handsome stranger who was staying for several days; Freyja learned this when she joined him and her mother for breakfast in front of the fire.

"Freyja, Tahir has been telling me such tales. And what a lover he is. He has learned many things from his travels," Arndis smiled and patted Tahir's butt as she spoke. "I can only hope you will know such pleasure, perhaps even the mighty passion."

"Indeed," thought Freyja, as she reflected on the night before with a weak smile. She had experienced no pleasure. She hoped that Sven would remember their encounter. If he did remember and did reciprocate her advances, then they, as well as the village, would have a good future, according to the divination. They would begin the wedding negotiations, but she did not feel hopeful, she felt nervous. She had so many questions to ask Sven, but they had never really talked. Their marriage and future life together were built on assumptions.

What if he did not acknowledge their romance? It would be difficult without a father or male relative to be a *fastnandi* and assert her rights in negotiating a marriage contract. Her mother might not even be allowed to make a contract for her. His well-off family might even insist that she not be Sven's wife, but only a concubine because of their dissimilar stations in life. Their farm had many cattle and slaves as well. She knitted her brow, doubt creeping in. These thoughts made her head hurt and she clutched her stomach.

"And you Freyja, did the night bring warmth to your loins?" Tahir asked with a wink. His smile lit up his face and he seemed sincerely interested.

"Freyja is special," responded her mother quickly. "She has a different path than most girls in our village. She is already promised to one of our people, but has yet to be with him."

Freyja saw Tahir's look of confusion and hurriedly interrupted, "Our old woman cast the runes and revealed our prophecy. Sven and I must come together and have children to bring good fortune to our village. The problem has been that Sven will not be a man."

Tahir laughed, "Oh, so he has problems?" and he lifted his finger and then bent it.

"No," Freyja snapped," he just has not been really interested in making this come true, yet. Perhaps he does not believe in such childish old tales as I do."

"Well, perhaps I can give you some tips on how to make him interested," Tahir batted his eyelashes and rolled his shoulder.

"NO," both women said loudly at once.

"All right, all right. Since this sounds sacred to you both, I will leave the subject alone. Perhaps you will show me your farm and where I can hunt for some meat." This suggestion set both women at ease and Arndis took Tahir for a walk around the farm. "Goats and chickens? This is enough for you?"

"We are but two women to manage these animals. We have vegetables in the garden and forage for much in the woods. It is fine for us," Arndis said shortly and pursed her lips while looking down, a bit embarrassed. She had never felt so with the local men. "Also, Freyja traps many rabbits."

"Ah yes, Freyja has the traps." Tahir was eager to change the subject, having understood Arndis' embarrassment. "Here she is to show me," he spoke, relieved. "Freyja, I would like to see where you trap and hunt."

"I make snares to trap the many rabbits that live in our forest. I do not really hunt as I have only my knife and no skills in hunting or warfare," Freyja said with downcast eyes. She raised her eyes and motioned for him to follow when her mother pointed with her chin toward the forest.

So, you know nothing of the weapons of hunting or war?" Tahir asked. He had known all her people to be well versed in such, men and women.

Freyja spoke over her shoulder as she led him to the path. "I have had no father, uncle, or brother to teach me," she answered simply. "We have nothing on the farm, but knives, axes, and tools."

"Even so," replied Tahir. He ran in front of her into a clearing. "You should know how to defend yourself." He

37

faced Freyja and took his knife out. "Take your knife and hold it as you would to fight me."

Freyja almost laughed, but the idea sobered her. She took her knife into her right hand and faced Tahir. He then proceeded to show her a defensive stance and some simple movements to evade the attack of another with a knife. "Be ready," Tahir yelled as he thrust his knife at Freyja. She jumped straight back and Tahir narrowly missed her. "You must watch my eyes and my body and be ready to move away." It seemed to become a bit easier until she tried to be the attacker. Again and again she failed to get her knife near Tahir's body. She became discouraged and it must have shown on her face. "You will become better with practice. Now, show me how you use your knife on the rabbits," Tahir requested.

Freyja was happy to take him to the woods to check her rabbit snares. The first snare was empty, but Tahir saw some other tracks nearby. He motioned Freyja to be silent and they ducked through the undergrowth to sneak up on a wild boar. It was bigger than any of the pigs at the neighbor's farms with its snout and gray skin covered in dirt. It was snorting loudly and was so intent on digging that it did not notice their approach. Tahir stealthily climbed a low tree branch and dropped upon the boar. He wrapped his strong legs around the animal and rode it while he struggled to get his knife to its throat. Squeals mixed with oaths for several minutes until the blade found the artery. When the boar stopped squealing and running, Tahir was a mess of scratches and blood from both himself and the boar. One of his legs was trapped under the massive body which had him pinned.

"Help me, little one. This boar is being a bit too amorous for me," Tahir said with his charming grin. He pushed while Freyja pulled to roll the boar off his leg. Then he raised one arm and Freyja reached her hand to his to pull him up off the ground. Tahir looked at the boar and rubbed his hands together with satisfaction, "Ah, yes. This is a good end to our hunt."

Freyja was filled with admiration and joy. This was a great feat that would feed them well and even provide trade on the next market day. They butchered it there and between the two of them were able to carry it back to the farm. "Mother, come and see," Freyja called out as they approached the farm. Arndis ran out the door and down the steps when she heard and greeted them joyfully.

"Oh my, oh my, look what you have brought," she repeated over and over again. Finally, Freyja suggested that Arndis bathe Tahir so she would both shut up and have something to do. Arndis brought Tahir inside to seat him at the table. She began to tenderly wash Tahir with a bowl of warm water and her cloth, discovering that most of the blood was from the boar. She kissed the spots as they became clean as he recounted the hunt for her. Their eyes never left each other and it seemed apparent that they would soon be back in Arndis's bed.

Freyja hummed cheerfully while she busied herself with cooking the boar. It had to be cut to fit on the spit over the fire and she worked on slicing the rest to dry. What a great day, food for a week or two for themselves, then as much for trade, and a happy mother! Indeed, when she looked back to the table, it had been abandoned, leaving the rag and bowl behind.

Then she thought about her own love life and the good fortune of the day faded from her mind. Her simple wish to fulfill the prophecy with Sven seemed much more complicated now. A girlish desire for love and passion had been turned into the reality of laws for marriage contracts and futures. She had never before really thought about the details surrounding her part of the prophecy and now, they began to dizzy her.

Well, she would just have to wait. With a sigh, she closed her eyes and fervently prayed to the gods that the next day would bring a response from Sven.

When the next day dawned Freyja determined to seek some advice from the Old One. She grabbed some bread and went to tend the animals. Chores done, she left the farm just as she heard Arndis and Tahir giggling through the open window. She sighed and wondered if she and Sven would ever know such happiness. How did Sven feel and what were his thoughts? Should she force him to speak of such things or should she wait, properly, for him to bring up the negotiations talk? Such worries made her head ache. She hurried her steps.

Where the three roads met, the usual market spot, she took the easterly path. A turn to the right led her over some wagon ruts and soon brought her to the farm of the Old One's family. A boy was chopping firewood and looked up to smile and wave as she approached the house. "Good day," Freyja called out. "I have come to speak with the Old One." The boy pointed into the woods at a small hut. Freyja waved her thanks.

The small pit house had smoke coming from the roof hole, but had no door. A blanket covering the doorway was lifted as she approached. "I felt you near, Little Freyja," the old one smiled as she pointed to the fire. She sat on a stool and motioned for Freyja to sit. Freyja used her hands to sit as her eyes adjusted to the dark. Seated on the ground, Freyja had to look up as if the Old One were on a high seat, as appropriate for a seeress. This vantage point made it so that she was also able to look about the hut and satisfy her curiosity.

The wattle walls were hung with necklaces, ells of cloth, feathers, and skins on bits of branches sticking out. Perhaps trade items that had been brought to her. There were baskets brimming with what seemed to be herbs stacked all around the woman on her seat and she reached for one. She pulled some leaves and crumpled them over the fire. They flared when they hit the flames and a sweet smoke filled the hut. She turned her face to Freyja and raised one eyebrow in a question.

"I have come to ask of the prophecy," Freyja began. The Old One put out her hand, palm up, and Freyja reached into her bag. She handed out boar meat, bread, and a baked root. The Old One took them gleefully, putting them in her lap, and broke off a bit of bread to eat. She chewed happily, ignoring Freyja as she shredded some of the boar. She

41

ate the boar together with the bread, loudly chewing and smacking her lips.

Freyja opened her mouth several times to speak, but closed it in haste each time. She must have made a sound because the Old One looked up each time in disgust. Finally, the Old One pulled a cloth from the wall to wrap her food and put it on the ground. She wiped her mouth with her hand, then reached out to lift Freyja's chin. She stared long and looked deeply into her eyes. "Your question?"

"What is meant of the rune telling?" Freyja blurted out.

The Old One dropped Freyja's chin roughly, knitted her brow, and smirked as if she thought Freyja an idiot. "When Freyja and Sven couple?" the Old One asked incredulously. "When the man and the woman come together...," she made some rough gestures with her hands. "You have seen the farm animals... And from this, children are born."

"I know this," Freyja wailed, holding her jaw. "I know that the village will prosper as a result, but will I prosper? Will I be happy? Will Sven and I know the mighty passion?" Freyja's voice was pitched and she was on the verge of tears.

The Old One looked astonished with the questions. She gazed into the fire then reached into a basket to pull out some more herbs. She put the herbs into the kettle she had on the fire and reached for two cups. After a few moments of silence, she dipped some liquid from the kettle into the cups and handed one to Freyja and then sipped her own. Freyja sipped and sighed loudly. Each time she sighed the Old One scowled.

Finally, the Old One spoke, "I shall consult the runes." She reached around, behind herself and brought out a leather pouch that she then held out to Freyja. "You will draw one out." She nodded to Freyja to put down her cup and to put out her hand. The Old One dropped the bag, grabbed Freyja's hand, and pricked Freyja's fingertip with something sharp. A claw-like hand grasped the girl's wrist while wrinkled fingers squeezed her fingertip to bring a drop of blood. The Old One brought the leather pouch up again and held it open for Freyja. Freyja reached in to pull out a rune. She showed it to the Old One.

"Ah, Raido, the rune of travel. You must soon go on a journey," the Old One hissed the words. She spread a cloth beside her. Her white head bent over the bag as she whispered and breathed into it. She then dumped the contents of the bag on the cloth. "You will need to make offerings to the gods to find your answers. The lady Freyja will need offerings of her tears to speak of love and passion. The lord Freyr will need offerings of boar's blood to speak of the abundance of children and prosperity."

Freyja practically laughed with joy and relief as she smiled. "This is easy enough," she said. "The forest is filled with both. Tell me how I should make the offerings."

The old woman looked seriously into Freyja's eyes for a long moment, then looked again at the runes. "When Sven leaves for the viking, you will go to find these things and bring them back to me. You will walk toward the rising sun and make your camp above the tree line on *Grjot Fell*, the rocky peak. You will take what things you need and also take a man that you may not need." The Old One stood and waved her hand at Freyja and at the door. Freyja stood to leave with a puzzled look on her face.

"I am not sure..." Freyja began. The Old One pushed her toward the door and followed her into the sunshine. She stretched her back and smiled at Freyja, then turned away and began to walk toward the farm house.

The woman turned back. "Give your mother my greetings. I hear the gods have given her a gift of love from the south," the Old One chuckled and wiggled her hips. Freyja watched with her mouth open and the Old One walked spryly to the farm house greeting her grandchildren with hugs and laughter.

Chapter Five

A few mornings later, Arndis' farm was awakened by Og storming up the steps into the house. "Hail, the farm," he panted. "It seems that Tahir has friends in the village. They need him to join them at once. They came to my hall and paid me good coin to deliver this message," Og shouted. He followed his sour greeting with a yawn. The visitors had roused the Headman and sent him to encourage Tahir to leave while they traded in the village. "You should dress quickly and go," Og yelled at Arndis' door. He started to lift the skin drape, out of habit, and then let it fall as he stepped back.

Arndis held Tahir's hand as she led him out of her room and made a wonderful show of a tearful goodbye. "I will miss you, my Moor lover. Peace and health only," said Arndis holding his face between her hands. Tahir whispered close to her ear as they embraced. Then she kissed Tahir slowly and deeply while Og rolled his eyes. When they stepped apart the last thing to touch was one of their hands.

Freyja sat at the table and watched this. Then she followed the group to the door wondering if this farewell kiss might, at least in part, be real as she yelled her own friendly goodbyes to Tahir. He had truly been a cordial and helpful guest. As he started down the path she wondered aloud if they would ever see him again. "Maybe we will see Tahir next year."

"Not likely, but perhaps I will stay for the day," said Og with a smile toward Arndis.

"And what have you brought to trade?" asked Arndis.

"Nothing today, but I will bring...," Og's voice trailed off.

"What is in your bundle?" inquired Arndis as she reached to look inside the fabric he had set on the table.

"Only some bread, cheese, and meat Helga wanted me to trade in the village. I cannot give it away."

"Then I have nothing to give away," smirked Arndis. She had both hands on her hips.

"But, just think of the milk cow I will bring for Freyja," he bellowed. He grabbed Freyja at the waist from behind and thrust into her. Freyja swatted his arms and stomped on his feet. She hissed at him while Arndis pulled him off and pushed him through her doorway.

The women stood side by side, as Og ambled toward the bed, both of them rolling their eyes. Freyja's eyes followed him like daggers. They turned back to the kitchen area to sit at the table.

"Now we have a moment," Arndis noted. "Tell me how things went with Sven the other night. You were cozy on his lap when we left. I thought it a good sign."

Freyja took a deep breath, and her shoulders drooped. "I showed him of my willingness, but of Sven, I do not know," pouted Freyja. "I do not know if the prophecy has any true meaning, at least for me."

"Well, many others have said the same thing lately, including Og. You will need to think on this," said Arndis with a sigh while patting her daughter's shoulder.

"But what do you think, mother?" asked Freyja.

"I? I am no longer sure. Most of childbearing age make their choice quickly, but many people have thought that the foretelling makes things different for you and Sven. He should already be talking with his family about a bride price equal to your dowry and gifts to give you the morning after your wedding. The morning gifts should be of value from his prosperous family. Enough to keep you well in household goods and perhaps farm animals. We have put away your dowry, so have no need to worry in that regard. Perhaps you can talk to Sven and see what he thinks," replied Arndis. She looked pleased with the discussion and patted the table, turning to rise.

"Sven does not talk," said Freyja grimly as she slumped on the bench. She watched her mother walk to lift the drape to her room, with a sour look.

Freyja left the farm to pass a somber day in the forest. She sought what medicinal plants they might use and trade but had a hard time keeping her mind on the task. She found herself sitting on a log or a rock and drawing aimlessly with a stick in the dirt. She tried to keep a look out for food items plentiful enough for market. The boar meat had cooked well over the fire, and they were enjoying it. The rest was drying and would go to the next market day. The meat and today's wild crafting could make it a profitable day for them. Only after one of her breaks to sit did she finally find some mushrooms, but would have to decide if they were to be taken to market or used at home.

She returned home after sunset to find no one about. She ate and went to her room. Freyja had time to reflect, lying on her soft sleeping skins. She thought of how it might be to have Sven with her. Two people with a fire for each other, as she imagined the "goings on" between her mother and her customers on the other side of her wall, would make her own bed warm. She let her hands explore her body and imagined her hands belonged to Sven. She would teach him how and where to touch her to bring her pleasure. Often, she heard how to bring men pleasure, but the recent visitor to her mother had spoken of bringing pleasure to the woman as well. She would guide Sven's hands, and they would both enjoy each other. She skillfully pleasured herself, as she hoped Sven might, until she erupted in joyful waves and then fell into a deep sleep.

Freyja woke to the sound of her mother pounding on the wall above her bed. It was dark except for a soft glow at her window. "Freyja, go to the barn. Something is bothering the animals. Go see."

"Yes, yes." Freyja sat up groggily and wrapped her shawl around her shoulders. She yawned and rubbed her eyes as she crossed the yard to the barn in the waning moonlight. It was probably just a stupid goat who had gotten itself stuck somewhere. She pushed the door open and stepped into darkness. After she shut the door and stood awhile her eyes adjusted to the dim moon light. There in front of her was a milk cow!

Suddenly, she was grabbed from behind. Her arms were pinned to her sides, and she felt hot lips on her neck, the breath smelled of mead. She felt a rough hand fumble to pull her night dress up and grab her ass. Panic rose in her chest. Her throat tightened. A milk cow? Had her mother accepted on her behalf? Had she been sold into the life of her mother?

She was pushed forcefully forward at the waist and now felt firm skin against her skin. She started to kick and found herself flipped around and on her back in the hay. A form hovered briefly above her and was then on top of her roughly pushing her legs apart. In the dark she could see no more than the outline of a man. Her hands pushed against his chest, but her strength was no match for the aggressor. The cow made some noise shifting and the man's head lifted. At that moment Freyja pushed the heal of her hand up into the base of his nose.

"Ow, by *Thor*, Freyja." The form fell upon one arm as his other hand went to his nose. He then rolled beside her so she could see the face in the dim light.

"Sven," she gasped and was flooded with a multitude of emotions. She rolled on her side to look at him. Tears of anger filled her eyes. She slapped his face. He looked dumbfounded.

"If you would only ask for my love, you would save yourself pain," Freyja shook her head in wonder. They lay in silence for a few moments then realization spread across her face and could be heard in her voice, "Sven, you are here for me." She felt her heart almost burst with the conflicting emotions of relief and passion. She stroked his face gently saying, "Poor Sven." She leaned over to kiss him deeply and they embraced tightly. She pulled him close to her body and rolled over on top of him remembering the stones upon her altar.

Her legs slid to his sides, wanting to take him in. Her arms searched for his shoulders to pull him close, both for comfort and desire. Her bosom swelled to press against his chest where they breathed as one. He met her and they found a rhythm together. She brought her hips to meet his and felt a new urge, a wanting, a deep need. She did not need to understand it, but let it take her. The pleasure she had not felt during their first encounter was now real. Each kiss was as sweet as warm mead and intoxicated her with joy. They found immense pleasure together and fell back in the hay, breathless, into each other's arms.

Freyja drifted off then felt herself on her back with Sven kissing and suckling on her breasts. This new sensation made the tiny hairs on her belly tingle. The moisture on her skin made little bits of skin shiver and she felt muscles deep inside contract. Sven grabbed her hand and put it on his member as he rolled on top of her. She felt him enlarge and guided him inside of her slowly to experience the movements with a new understanding. Once again, they moved until they burned together with a fire that almost consumed them.

The inn matki munr, the mighty passion, as I had with your grandfather. People may speak of it still, whispered her grandmother's spirit.

Freyja woke with a smile on her face, the milk cow nuzzling her foot. Her prayers to the gods had been answered and the prophecy begun, this time in earnest. She was thrilled to know such passion with Sven. Freyja rubbed her belly, sure that she wanted to know this feeling again and again. She reached out a hand to search for Sven and felt nothing. Rolling over she opened her eyes, letting them wander the barn.

Sven was nowhere to be seen, and she frowned. A feeling of unease flooded her. She rose to feed the goats, the horse and the new cow. She opened the door so the animals could go into the corral and then froze. A milk cow? The audacity of Og! She gritted her teeth and set her jaw with indignation. Rage boiled up inside her and she stormed toward the house.

The floors echoed with her stomping up the steps and inside. She barged into her mother's room to confront Arndis and Og. "You will need to take your cow," Freyja waved her arm toward the door. "I am not for sale. I am bound to fulfill the prophecy," Freyja shouted at Og, "Take your cow and go." She gestured to the door.

"Oh, little one, you have come to join us," Og patted the bed and scooted over to make room for her.

"No, I am not here to join you," she spat. Take your cow and go," Freyja repeated forcefully.

"What does she talk about? Go with a cow?" Og's expression was confused. He shrugged, looking over his shoulder at Arndis as if she might translate.

Arndis found her voice as she woke and understood the situation. "No, no, my sweet. The cow is not for you, and it is not from Og." Arndis got up to hold her daughter's shoulders while she looked into her face. "The cow is from Tahir. He sent it from the village to pay for his time here. It came while you were in the forest yesterday." She reached up to pull hay from Freyja's hair. "Have you been playing in the hay so early?"

Now Og was interested and sat up. "A cow in your barn? Now what can I offer for Freyja?" he said with a sad pout to his lips.

Freyja pushed him back down on the bed, with her foot on his belly. "You have nothing worthy of offering and besides you are too late. The prosperous future is unfolding!" She ended her triumphant speech by sticking out her tongue at Og, retracting her foot, and trouncing out of the room.

"My daughter," Arndis raced after her. By the cooking fire she grabbed Freyja's arm and spun her around. She searched the girl's face. "You and Sven?" she asked.

"Yes, I am only for Sven and Sven will be only for me," she said flushing.

"Ah, yes. You are now for Sven, but men, they are different," said Arndis shaking her head with a half-smile. "They may come and go, as they travel and trade."

"The gods have told me that if I am for Sven, then Sven is also for me. Our mating will bring good fortune for all of our village lands. It is done." Freyja pulled away. She grabbed her overdress from the peg and walked out of the house and into the woods with a purposeful stride.

Og came out of Arndis's room rubbing his belly. "So, Freyja's ripe fruit has been picked. I would like to have tasted her sweetness. Perhaps in the years to come." He sighed as he sat on a bench at the table.

Arndis held up a hand, "Enough, she is the one to decide and she says she will only be for Sven. She thinks she knows what the future has in store for her. I did not think this would be my life, but look at me," Arndis's arms spread wide.

"So, what did you think? That you would live forever with your prince, and he would give you more coins? That your parents would never sicken to tie you to the farm?" Og replied.

Arndis sat heavily on the bench across the table from Og. "You are right. A woman alone with a child and parents to care for has little choice," she nodded her head in acquiescence.

"But just think, if you did not have this life, you would not have me," Og grinned showing his missing tooth. "I would not bring you cheese or chickens or cows...," he stopped in mid-sentence, his eyes narrowing. "So, where did Tahir get a cow?"

A slow smile came to Arndis's lips. "Tahir sent word that he met an angry woman on the path who was looking for her husband. The husband was supposed to have traded some bread and cheese and meat for the family that morning. He had not returned so she was taking matters into her own hands. I wonder who that could have been?" asked Arndis too innocently.

Og stood up suddenly bumping his belly against the table. He mumbled curses about wives, women, and milk cows. He grabbed his clothes and hurried out the door and down the steps toward the path. He mumbled as he dressed while walking then yelled, over his shoulder, loudly enough for Arndis to hear. "The women of this village have conspired with the gods against me."

Chapter Six

The house was still and Arndis was alone. Sitting at her table she allowed herself the luxury of daydreaming. It was not often that she found herself in this situation. Either she was "entertaining" a man or with Freyja. Her thoughts turned to the past and Freyja, her golden-haired daughter, of strong body and willful temperament. She had always been a help. Freyja had kept Arndis going during the "winter of the sickness". Her little toddler arms had encircled her mother's neck and brought comfort when the stress of caring for both her sick parents seemed too much. Arndis's mother died that winter and she had quickly slipped into her mother's role of caring for her father and then caring for the farm. Once her father had recovered it was spring and he was off with the raiding parties. They settled into a routine of winter and raiding for several more years and then one autumn Arndis's father came home with a mortal wound. He did not leave to go raiding that spring, but instead was given a warrior's fiery funeral in the snow.

She shivered as she remembered standing in the snowdrift as flakes continued to fall around her. She had stepped closer to the pyre to warm herself, putting both her hands up with palms facing the fire as the sparks rose. It looked as if the sparks were rising from her fingertips into the clear night sky. Her eyes followed the rising sparks to watch them join the stars above to form a ship which carried her father's spirit away.

Arndis realized that she had let her old life go, with the sparks, floating away in the night and sighed. She often fell into wistful dreaming of the life she might have had with her one true love, Freyja's father. Brion would have surely kept her warm. They had sent him home before any knew of Freyja. Would he have been a good father to Freyja? Would he have taken them back to his prosperous clan holdings? Life with her lover in a faraway land held much fuel for dreams, but it did not take long for her to discover that the oldest profession in the world was a sure reality for keeping food on their table. It was now her reality.

In the meadow, Freyja's thoughts also drifted to the past as she thought of her mother and the life she led. She did not understand how her mother could feign passion with every man who showed up at their door. She could associate passion with only one, with Sven. She wanted to conquer him with every physical encounter. Even last time, when Sven had seemed to be the aggressor, she felt that she had held the power as he succumbed to her offerings. He could not help himself but to give in to his own passions for her body. She had felt the power of her womanhood at that moment and knew that she could use it to her advantage with Sven. Perhaps her mother knew of this power as well, the thrill of conquest. Maybe it had helped Arndis reconcile herself to a life without true love. She wanted to know more about the real passion that her mother had once felt, perhaps with her own father, and decided to return home. She found her mother at the table with her head cradled on her arms, weeping. She touched her on the shoulder and Arndis jumped noticeably. Freyja put her arms around her mother's neck.

"Freyja. I was just remembering you hugging me, like this, as a little one!" exclaimed Arndis. She sniffed loudly.

"Why do you cry, Mother?" Freyja asked with a worried look.

"I'm thinking about losing people," sighed Arndis with barely a smile. She wiped her eyes with the back of her hands, "My mother and then my father...," her voice trailed off.

"And my father, what of him?" probed Freyja.

"He too," replied Arndis. "The loss of him as well."

"Will you tell me of him now? Have I ever seen him? Do I look like him? Did you feel *inn matki munr* with him? Did you know the mighty passion?"

"Freyja, enough!" Arndis held up her hand for a long moment. "It is time for you to know. As a child you did not need to know, and tongues wagging may have spoiled the prophecy. You are now a woman and will understand the ways of love." Arndis sat taller, took a deep breath, and began, "It was with the last raid of the season, your father came. Your grandfather's ship barely made it home before our shore was ice bound. But they came home triumphantly with many tales and goods and one captive. There was arguing among the people about what we would do with him. Some said he was a perfect slave to use for the winter and then to sell. Others said we should keep him until the ice broke, then send to demand a ransom from his wealthy family."

"The captive was my father?" interrupted Freyja breathlessly.

"Aaaah!" glowered Arndis in frustration, then continued. "So, it was decided to keep him for one winter and then to ask for ransom. If the ransom offered was not enough, then he would be sold as a slave. At first, he was kept in a tent from the raid, near the village. Families took turns bringing food to him and many of us girls volunteered as we were curious about this strange boy."

"Boy, my father was a boy?" Freyja laughed in nervous amazement.

"We are not born old, Freyja. Yes, he was a boy about the age you are now. I was perhaps the age of Sven. I would set the food I brought just inside the tent and then watch him from the opening. He was oddly beautiful, with dark hair and his blue eyes were very much like yours. He was taller than I, as you are. His body was slender, but very strong." Freyja looked down at her own strong, muscled body. "He had obviously worked or was a warrior in his homeland, though everything about him seemed gentle, not like the rough men in our village. Helga called him 'skinny as a stick' that first day when she brought water to wash off his blue Woad markings. He seemed willing to be washed, almost like he was expecting it. Being older than me, she laid claim to him and knelt down and tried to arouse him, but he grabbed her wrists. She had liked his fire, but he would not have her so she said she would not help with him again."

Freyja asked, "Do you mean Helga, Og's wife?" Her eyes were wide with disbelief. She shook her head and giggled.

"Again, Freyja, those who are now old were once young," Arndis said softly with a far-away look in her eyes. She shook her head and returned to the story, "When the snows came, there was much arguing about Brion. Who would take him?"

Freyja silently mouthed the name, "Brion."

"Finally, my father offered our barn and our table to care for the boy, but only for the winter. My father told my mother that the decision was made no matter how much she rolled her eyes. I was given the job of watching after him. At first, I was angry. Being the only surviving child of the family, I had enough work. Then I became curious about him."

"What about passion with him, *inn matki munr*?" urged Freyja.

Arndis chuckled. "Well, my dear one, that came later. I would bring his food and he would ask me to stay by patting the hay next to him. We began to learn the others words and soon we could share stories. I took him out of the barn to walk the farm and the woods. He began to help me with my rabbit snares. He even took on the care of the goats since he was with them in the barn. We spent the whole winter laughing much. When the ice began to break up, the men prepared to travel back to his home to demand ransom. My father said that I could be relieved of the burden of "this animal", but I said I was used to caring for one more animal and it would be no trouble."

"You called him an animal?" Freyja's face reflected the question.

"Yes," Arndis looked down in embarrassment. "I wanted to show no feelings for him."

Freyja broke in, "But you had feelings?"

"Yes, I felt my heart quicken each time he looked at me." Arndis blushed uncharacteristically, then went on. "After the men left that spring, I let my feelings be known. My mother had left for market day, so I brought Brion to my bed (yours now) and took him."

"You took him?" Freyja asked somewhat intrigued and relieved.

"Well, it was clear that he wanted me, as well," Arndis smiled slightly.

"Was your passion great?" pressed Freyja.

Arndis smiled and nodded, "Ah yes it was, that is why I chose your name. I hope you will someday know this feeling and feel like the goddess of passion yourself. The Lady works with love and sex and will share with you if you call upon her. She shows us that searching for love is honorable as she searched for her husband, Odr. Her tears of red gold are often found in the bark of the trees." Arndis reached out for Freyja's hand and brought it to her heart.

There were tears in her eyes again and she heaved a great sigh. "Brion was torn from me with the pain of a scab pulled from a wound. There was nothing I could do. Even if we had known of you, he most likely would have been returned for the ransom. I would have been quickly married to some man, but I would have still longed for him. My heart still feels this loss, but you..., you have always made me happy."

Chapter Seven

This new morning Freyja felt different, somehow new herself. Hearing her mother's story gave her strength and she lifted her chin, squared her shoulders. She thought how like her mother she was, boldly laying claim to her man. Freyja, child of the mighty passion of Arndis and Brion. She tried the name of her father on her tongue, "Brion," she said softly. Now, she knew more about her father and mother and strangely, about herself.

She did her chores and then wandered to the woods. She had no plans, but to enjoy the sunshine. She soon met up with others doing the same. In a clearing, a group of young men were enjoying some mead, telling stories, and wrestling in the grass.

"Daughter of *Njord*, hail and well met. We have mead and lust to share," yelled Karle. Another boy held out his drinking horn then, realizing it was empty, threw it down. The others found the same. "We would have shared mead, now all we have is lust," Karle went up to Freyja and put one arm around her.

"No, no," said another through puckered lips, "Freyja is for Sven."

"Sven has said nothing and we tire of waiting. What do you say Freyja, will you give it to me?" Karle grabbed Freyja's hips.

"You are right, I keep myself for Sven," she pushed Karle's hands off.

"Then you miss out on great sweetness," Karle kissed the air at her. The group of boys began to wander off joking and rough-housing.

"Yes, I know," called Freyja after them, "your mead is gone." Freyja heard their voices reduce to a murmur and turned her attention to the clearing. One drinking horn had been left at the base of a large tree.

"Something has come of this meeting, at least," she thought. She bent down to retrieve the horn and saw Sven behind a great tree. His lean, muscular body stretched out in the shade, an obvious casualty of too much mead and sun. Freyja tip toed to his side and knelt. His long blonde hair spread out like the roots of the tree his head was nestled between. Freyja thought of the stories of *Yggdrasil*, the world tree, at the center of the nine worlds. Sacred to all the gods, it connects everything.

Sven was central to Freyja's world, here and now. His pants lay in a damp pile nearby and she thought the boys must have been swimming this day. His hands were clasped together on his chest as he lay sound asleep on his back. Freyja felt a shiver of anticipation as she reached over to gently lift Sven's tunic.

She was not disappointed when she unveiled his treasures. It had been too dark to see him on their previous encounters and she looked hungrily at him. She marveled at his construction and how it all worked. She reached out tentatively with her fingertips hoping to discover his textures and form.

Sven cautiously assessed the situation as he slowly opened one eye, for a faint smile crossed his lips and then he quickly feigned sleep once again. He loved the attentions of this beautiful woman but wondered if she really wanted him or just the prophecy. All everyone spoke of was the damn foretelling. His mind was full of doubts and wondering, but his senses tingled with the heady smell of her and he braced himself.

Freyja felt a warmth growing in her belly and it soon spread to her loins. Her only focus was Sven. She encircled his manhood with her strong fingers and he reacted fully, in kind. She was again flooded with a sense of power. Now, taking advantage of Sven's reaction was her driving goal. With lightning quick movements, she pulled up her skirts and straddled Sven's hips. Once again, she felt how right it was as their parts were meeting. Sven stirred and she felt a guilty pleasure in her belly. She was taking him.

Her senses heightened and she could feel muscles deep inside her react when she arched her back to ride him. A great urge filled her and she leaned forward savagely grabbing Sven's hips to pull him into her. Their hearts beat together, chest to chest. "Sven, Sven," she spoke his name like a plea. She felt like a bear climbing a tree and could hear herself growl and groan. He answered with his own moans, a confirmation that he was no longer asleep.

Sven threw his arms around her, stroked her back and thrust his hips into her. "Freyja, Freyja," he murmured clutching her hips firmly. She could feel his fingers denting into her skin, but the pressure was pleasant, even welcomed. To be touched by the one she loved!

Her body shuddered and she gasped as she came to understand the fullness of her pleasure. All of Sven's muscles tensed. He too came to know his pleasure with muscles tensed and breath held. They relaxed and held each other warmly, breathing heavily. Freyja sat up slowly when Sven let go and they shared a smoldering look, locked onto each other's eyes.

Sven cleared his throat and it seemed that he might speak, when they heard snorts and chuckles from the edge of the clearing. The boys must have returned and witnessed at least some of their passionate gyrations. Freyja jumped up to smooth her skirts and Sven pulled down his tunic. They both tried to look nonchalant, but Freyja felt like her cheeks were on fire.

"I am indeed too late to claim you Freyja. Though it seems to be Sven who has been claimed," Karle whooped and slapped his thigh. "You two are well mated with much groaning and thrusting."

Two of the boys grabbed each other at the hips and thrusted and moaned together. "Oh, Freyja," said one. "Oh, Sven," said the other.

"Sven, I would ask you to come with us and tell us of your conquest, but it seems that Freyja should join us men," joked Karle. He grabbed Sven by the arm and pulled him forcefully up off the ground. He threw Sven's pants at him, laughing. "You are now Freyja's whore," Karle slapped Sven on the back as they walked away with the gang. Sven was the attention of the boys as they joked with him and cheered his feats, walking toward the village.

Freyja stood with her mouth hanging open, watching Sven disappear down the path without a backward look. Shaking her head, she resigned herself to the knowledge that soon the whole countryside would know that she and Sven had been together. Some would be happy that they might be nearer fulfilling the prophecy, and Og and some of the girls might be disappointed. All would be watching the timing now. Negotiators for the marriage contract, bride-price, dowry, morning gift would all need to be agreed upon. They would each need to acquire a sword and a ring to give the other at the wedding. All these details must be worked out before a wedding, on a *Frigga's* day, could be set and then one moon of honey mead made ready.

Chapter Eight

Several torturous days passed and again she heard nothing from Sven. She longed to touch his body and feel the tingle of pleasure she had so recently learned. She wished to take good advantage of the short time they had left. The days were lengthening and soon Sven would join most of the able-bodied men on a viking. They would be joining men from other villages to make up raiding parties to the Far Isle. From her vantage point on the cliff behind the farm house, Freyja could already see the local ship being outfitted for the arduous journey.

As a small child her grandmother held her to wave goodbye to her grandfather from the rocky prominence. She would imagine that he waved back even if her eyes could not be sure. Then she became the lookout, standing as tall as she could after her grandmother died, when she scrambled up each day to see if the ship had returned. When, after several long warm months, she saw it, she would call out loudly and pull her mother up to see. They would jump merrily astride their horse and start down the winding path that cut into the side of the fjord, hurrying to the sand below. They would run to hug her grandfather, greet the others and load the horse with the spoils destined for their house. Often *Afi* would press a gold piece into her small hands with the admonishment to put it into her dowry. Then the girls were sent back up the path while grandfather joined the men in the Mead House. He would wander home in the late hours that night or early the next morning and find his way to his bed. Only after he had rested well, would Arndis let Freyja pester her grandfather for his tales of adventure. She remembered the details as if through a fog, for he had died when she was still young. She caught herself wondering aloud, "Perhaps I will take the path to the beach to welcome Sven back from his adventures."

She turned to take stock of the farm. The goats and the cow were happily munching on the new grass near the house. She had protected the garden from their ever-hungry lips with a make-shift fence of logs; the animals would care for themselves. It was perfect sunny weather for washing clothes and a walk to the creek was something she always enjoyed.

She went inside to gather musty garments from the pegs on the walls. It made a large bundle for her basket. "I am washing at the creek," she yelled to her mother, but then remembered that Arndis had walked to the village to find some business. She hopped down the steps with a smile and began her long walk with purposeful and joyful steps.

Every trip through the woods was magical for her. She let her eyes linger on the varied colors of new green growth on trees and plants. They delighted her as much as she imagined they delighted the gods in their tending. A soft breeze stirred the branches and their movements created music and a dance just for her. She listened for the sounds of animals going about their lives. A scuttle, as bugs crossed the path, the buzz of honey bees. She would take note of their hive for her neighbors, the twins' family, who made mead. The bees always made more honey than they needed and her friends knew just how much to take to the benefit of both man and bee.

The creek was running high but there were still good rocks available to use for washing. She picked out a spot that was well situated except that the sun would be in her eyes. "Well," she thought, "my head will be down most of the time." She tucked up her skirts, grabbed a piece of clothing and stepped into the icy water. At this time of year, the water was snow melt and her feet would become almost numb. She breathed through the tingling pain and concentrated on rubbing out the grime in the cloth. With practiced movements she rubbed and beat the cloth on the rocks, then rinsed and wrung out the water. She started a pile of wet bundles on a large rock. The noise of the moving water filled her ears so she did not hear Sven creep up behind her. He touched her back and she froze while washing a moss green scarf that belonged to her mother.

Sven whispered in her ear, "Freyja is for Sven," and let his lips graze her neck. She felt his hands at her waist and his bare legs against her own. The warmth of his shins against the back of her calves was delicious. She breathed herself up and against him and closed her eyes as his arms encircled her waist.

He slowly lifted her skirts from behind and she could feel him against her buttocks. The touch of his skin began to warm her own, and a fire began to build between her thighs. He gently caressed her hips. His hand slid slowly between her thighs; he was patiently studying her anatomy. She leaned forward slightly resting her arms and chest on the almost waist high rock, the scarf dangling over the edge. She welcomed her lover and took in the warmth of the rock as she took in Sven.

She was frustrated that she could not see him, had no control, but his enthusiasm was contagious and she let herself fall under his spell. She clung to the boulder as she surely would have clung to Sven had she been facing him. There was only the movement of Sven to her and her to him. His strong hands were at her waist and supple thighs pressed firmly against hers. Even if words had been spoken, they could not have been heard above the music of the water.

Sven did not rush this time, but paused often to control himself. Freyja in turn felt frustrated, but it only increased her wanting, her hunger. It was as if she were climbing a mountain and was just shy of reaching the peak again and again. He was toying with her, like a cat with a mouse. Her eagerness could no longer wait. She took a large gulp of air and gritted her teeth. In an almost violent upheaval, she pushed with her arms and thrust her hips back vigorously to meet him. She could feel her muscles tighten and the roaring creek within her crested. The scarf she had been clutching tightly fell from her hand as her fingers spread involuntarily. Sven responded with an upheaval of his own and pushed as if they were to share the same body. Then he wrapped his arms around her waist and filled her with his passion. He breathed in her fragrance with his face close to her back, feeling full yet empty at the same time.

Freyja crumpled slowly onto the rock and Sven followed staying inside her. They rested this way for a few precious moments, breathing as one. She felt the vibrations of his breaths go through her as if they were her own. His sighs of pleasure echoing through her body encouraging her own voicing of pleasure as she hummed dreamily.

Then she felt him stand up. She reached back to fix her skirts and stood up shakily. She took the time to push her hair away from her face as she knew she would look flushed and breathless. She wanted to tell Sven so much. How she felt satisfied, how she wanted to plan more meetings, how they might have a future. She turned, to lean back against the boulder, with a radiant smile and he was nowhere to be seen.

Dazed, she slowly made her way to sit down upon the bank. Her feet were numb even if the rest of her was still tingling. This passion was a good sign, was it not? Sven had been the instigator. Clearly, he enjoyed their relationship. He had said, "Freyja is for Sven", but could he have just been repeating what everyone had said for years? What did he feel? Would he send his *fastnandi* to negotiate the bride price for their wedding? Or did he look down upon her and wait to offer her the payment of only twelve ell of cloth, for a bed-slave? After all, her family no longer had the reputation or representation of a warrior. Her standing among their people depended wholly on an old casting of the runes.

Glumly, she gathered the wet bundles and spread them out on bushes to dry. She felt as if she would dry up as well. She crumpled to the ground with her head in her hands. Then lay back on the grass and imagined herself a dry leaf blowing on the wind.

Her eyes closed and she dozed off. Freyja dreamed herself the goddess with the same name. Sven was a fallen warrior she had just chosen to enter her hall, *Sessrumnir*. She beckoned him, from her high seat, to come to her feet. She descended and took his hand to lead him to her table. They ate a decadent feast then roughly pushed it aside to climb upon the table to make passionate love. Freyja then pulled Sven to a massive and grandly soft bed where they made love again. Sven gave every pleasure to his goddess. His hands moved where she directed, and his kisses covered her body. He gave whatever she asked, and they both were satisfied. They lay entwined in the grand bed for long hours.

From there they watched as hundreds of silver children, round like the coin Tahir had shown her, sprang out of the floor of the hall and danced before them. Finally, at the end of their dance, each child in turn jumped into a treasure chest bound with gold. Sven, mesmerized by the dancers, crawled from the bed to look down at them.

Without looking at Freyja he stood and slowly went to them. He gazed down with love at the children, then closed the chest and held it to his breast. With an enchanted look upon his face, he walked out of *Sessrumnir* without a backward glance. The hall was silent and Freyja was alone.

Freyja woke up drooling from the corner of her mouth. The sun had slipped below the tree line and she quickly gathered the dry clothes in a daze, hoping to make it home before dark. She walked home, her brow knitted, pondering the dream and her day. She could make no sense of either. With a sigh, she lifted her feet heavily up the steps at sunset then put the basket of clothes on the table. Some root stew with a piece of dried boar was eaten in silence, alone on a bench.

"Freyja, is that you?" Arndis's voice sang from her room. "I am going back to the village. Have you seen my green scarf?"

Freyja's mouth twisted into a devious smile as she remembered the day. She stuffed one last piece of dried meat into her mouth and mumbled around it. "I have not seen it around here, Mother," she replied innocently on her way to bed.

Chapter Nine

F reyja woke to the sound of a horn. It was one long blast, a pause and then another long blast in a series of five. It was the call to load the ship for the outgoing raiding party. The sun was rising, then high tide would signal their departure. Freyja did not know how much time she had, but wanted to see Sven off. Seeing him might answer a question as yet unformed on her lips. Anxiously she did her chores then gathered what gifts she thought might be of use to the explorers.

"I am to the ship," she called to her mother as she straddled the horse with a bundle of plentiful roots and herbs. Upon the old steed she flashed back to the days of this same trek to meet her grandfather. The journey had always brought a rush of excitement to her chest. The goodbyes full of possibilities of the adventures beyond their shores. She set out at a fast pace nervous about getting there in time to see Sven depart. Would words pass between them? Would Sven even acknowledge her presence in the middle of the crowd? She wanted both outcomes and chewed her lip with anxiety.

Just at the bottom of the trail she could see the crowd giving up its men to the ship. Freyja kicked the horse and they galloped across the open beach. She jumped off, running at full speed to press her bundle into Sven's hands.

"*Frigga's* blessings on you, 'Unharmed go forth, Unharmed return, Unharmed safe home," she whispered breathlessly. She felt electricity pass between their warm fingers as they touched and longed to hold on to Sven's hands. He pulled his hands away with the bundle, met her eyes with a steady gaze and nodded, then clambered aboard.

"Ah, here is Freyja," Og announced loudly. He put an arm around her shoulders, "I will take good care of her while you are gone, Sven."

Sven's head swiftly jerked to face Og, "No," he barked as an order with one hand raised. In a split second he seemed embarrassed by his own boldness and his hand and eyes both went down quickly.

Freyja shrugged off Og's arm, "He has said it. You see, I am for Sven. No one else will take care of me." She crossed her arms under her breasts and held her head up high. She sent a burning scowl to Og and then flashed her biggest smile to Sven. A slight smile of pleasure and amusement was on his face.

A clamor arose as people began to push the boat off the beach and the oars were raised. There was much waving and many calls for good luck as they rose with the high tide and made off from the fjord beach. Freyja waved with enthusiasm and thought she saw Sven wave back. "You may get lonely the many months Sven is gone," Og offered with a matter-of-fact tone.

"Ehhh, did you not hear what Sven said? No!" Freyja shook her head and rolled her eyes at Og.

Another voice spoke up. "Well, just remember the prophecy. You would do well to honor it and finally bring prosperity to us all. Your house is not noted for closed legs and yours might be just as easily opened, at the right price," Helga spoke as she stepped close to Freyja, chin up and meeting her eyes in challenge.

"Og, your woman needs to be quiet. Perhaps you can fill her mouth. That might keep you both at home," Freyja practically spat the words. Helga's mouth gaped open and she raised a fist to Freyja, which Freyja grabbed with one hand. With the other arm, she picked up the small, short woman and shoved her into Og's arms. "Take care of **her**," Freyja said as she mounted her horse.

She decided to take the long way home and to ride first through the village. It was very quiet without the able-bodied men. The Mead House was almost empty. Just a small group of old or injured men sat about one table. "Freyja, come and tell us of the sailing," called old Klaus. "Did they catch the tide?" Freyja joined the men to tell them who was on the ship and how they had set off. "We hear you have coupled with Sven, is this true?"

Freyja sat up proudly, "Yes, I am for Sven."

"This is good, very good. The Old One was right. Now we can look forward to your *Frigga's* day wedding and better times," said Klaus.

"We all hope that Sven will come back safely, but just in case perhaps you should sleep with one of us to ensure the children of the prophecy," said another as he patted her behind.

"I thank you for your kind offer, but I will wait for Sven," said Freyja kissing his wrinkled cheek. "Now, have you mead to share or just talk?" They quickly passed her a drinking horn and she joked and flirted with them. The serving woman with long dark hair came to fill their cups and horns. She rested a hand lightly on old Klaus' shoulder and whispered in his ear as she looked at Freyja, smiling shyly. Klaus whispered back to her and patted her hand as she left.

Freyja looked at Klaus with a raised eyebrow. "The girl is from far away and speaks little of our language. She asked your name," Klaus said.

They drank, toasting the voyage and singing of old heroes. They praised the strength of her grandfather and the beauty of her grandmother, long ago. Freyja loved the stories of old and learned more about these men who had themselves been warriors and traders. Together their skills and knowledge were impressive.

Later Helga and Og walked in with some of the others who had been at the boat's departure. Helga started toward Freyja, but Og steered her toward a table as she glared at the young woman enjoying herself. They settled in to talk and drink with the others, but it was short lived. Helga was restless and her face reddened. She walked up behind Freyja to clap her on the shoulder.

"What did I tell you? Sven not a sunset gone and she is already acting like her mother," Helga snarled.

Freyja jumped to her feet and found them a bit unsteady, "Yes, I am like my mother. I am a strong woman who can care for a farm and someday a family. I will do what I have to do to survive, like she has. I will learn how to keep my man satisfied like she does. You know only how to whine and cannot even keep your man at home." Helga looked up furiously at Freyja and pushed with all of her might. Freyja fell back into the arms of an old man and passed out.

"Thank the gods for this gift, but I no longer know what to do with it," he joked.

"I, as Headman, will make sure she and her horse get home safely," offered Og a bit too quickly. Helga turned even more bright red, her eyebrows almost meeting her hairline. "It is the right thing to do, Helga. Now you should go home as well." Og threw Freyja over his shoulder and walked out with Helga nagging after him. "I will come home when I am ready to come home," Og bellowed to Helga. Og mounted Freyja's horse and another man handed Freyja up to him. He held her on his lap, with one hand, the bridle in the other for the journey. When they arrived at the farm, he yelled for Arndis, "Come out and help me with your child."

Arndis hurried down the steps to take Freyja from him. Og then dismounted and picked up the girl. "What has happened?" asked Arndis.

"Only too much mead," chuckled Og. "The old men filled their eyes with her as she drained them of their mead." Og carried her up the steps and then to her bed.

"And her blouse? Did the old men loose it?" asked Arndis suspiciously. She glared at Og, "Well, does she let old men undress her? I think not."

Og stammered, "I offered to bring her safely home, not leave her in the Mead House to be taken advantage of."

"So, you took advantage of her yourself?" Arndis pushed him out of Freyja's room. "You will go now," commanded Arndis as she walked him to the door and held it open.

"But I have brought coins," he said as a child not understanding. Arndis's eyes flashed quickly to the sparse kitchen larder and then back to Og. "And the sun is going down and I am on foot," Og whined.

Arndis drew herself taller, determined. "Then you will have to hurry," she said as she pushed him out the door and slammed it shut.

Arndis went to Freyja's side. She looked at the face of her sleeping daughter, no longer a child, but a woman. She sat down to cradle Freyja's head in her lap and stroked her hair while she sang. She remembered doing this so long ago and her heart filled with the pangs of regret. Regret for not having done this enough when Freyja was a child. Always there had been work on the farm, caring for her parents and later caring for the men, her business, her way of life. She cried as she sang and remembered.

"Mama," Freyja murmured, smiling, and hugging her mother, then drifted off to sleep again.

In the morning mother and daughter woke snuggled together as in days gone by. "Mother," Freyja squinted "did you come to the Mead House?"

"No little one."

"I don't remember coming home."

"Og brought you and the horse to the farm," Arndis did not mention Og's indiscretion.

"Well then where is Og?" Freyja looked around with concern.

"You needn't look. I threw him out," Arndis answered. Freyja looked at her mother as if she were crazy, but then sighed contentedly and closed her eyes to sleep some more, nestled peacefully next to her mother. Arndis let her sleep and later brought broth and cheese to her.

"Shall I get up and tend to the animals?" Freyja felt as if she were shirking her duties.

"No, it is done. I have had time this day. Do not worry," said Arndis as she joined Freyja once more.

Arndis felt more relaxed than she had in a long time. There would not be many customers with the raiding party gone and she might have worried about the thinning larder. But she also had time to take stock of what they did have. These two strong, healthy women had a milk cow and goats, a plentiful garden and time to devote to the farm. The women spent the whole day remembering stories and laughing until it was time to put the animals away. They combed and braided each other's long hair by the fire. They had not had time to indulge in this for quite a while and enjoyed new stylings as both were unmarried and wore their hair unbound. With grateful hugs they parted to a peaceful night's sleep.

Thus, began a joyful pattern for summer weeks. They would rise with the sun to care for the animals and then eat together. They worked on farm repairs and the garden, on sewing and crafts. They drank milk and made butter from the contented cow who gave plentifully. They made cheese from the goat's milk now that the kids were weaned. Freyja's rabbit snares were always full to supply them with stew meat and pelts. They even went to the creek together to do the wash.

Freyja's cheeks burned when she remembered the last time she had been there with Sven. She could feel his body next to hers in memories and it made her breath quicken.

"Freyja," Arndis asked "are you well? You seem flushed."

"It is . . . it is only the work of washing mother," Freyja stammered with a secretive smile.

"Ah, I was wondering if you might be with child?" Arndis asked with raised eyebrows.

"No mother, I know this is not so and will not be for some time as Sven is gone," Freyja stated matter-of-factly, though she absentmindedly touched her belly.

"Well, you would know, but I am starting to feel the prosperity of the prophecy coming true. We must be prepared for wedding negotiations before children anyway, but we are well and our needs are well met."

"Yes mother, I am happy too," she smiled at her mother. "Sven has been brought to me by the gods and when he returns the rest of the prophecy will unfold."

They sat on the creek bank in the sun while the laundry dried, spread out on the bushes. When they felt too warm, they decided to wash themselves and went in for a swim. The two women stripped and waded in to splash each other playfully. They dunked their heads and let the water carry their worries away downstream. They floated on their backs and watched the clouds in peaceful silence. Then they showed each other interesting stones and commented on the abundant fish. Next time they agreed, they would try to catch some. Freyja started to speak, but was silenced by an abrupt gesture from Arndis. Arndis submerged in the water up to her neck while pointing to the opposite bank. Freyja did the same when she saw the large mother bear with her cub approaching the creek. Silently they let the current carry them downstream away from the bears and under some low hanging branches.

From their hiding place they watched the bears fish and play in the water for a long time. Sitting still made the water feel colder and Freyja desperately wanted to find the sunshine. She began to move toward the bank and the sun with Arndis following. Bent over they crawled up the bank receiving scratches from branches on their backs. On the end of one of the branches was Arndis' green scarf. Arndis clutched it in her hand while she gave Freyja a disgusted look. Arndis' look made Freyja start to giggle and both women had to stifle their laughter so as not to draw the bears' attention. Luckily, they were downwind as well as downstream so the bears did not notice them and wandered leisurely off on the opposite bank.

With sighs of relief, both women watched the animals depart and made their way back upstream to their laundry and clothing. "Mother," Freyja spoke as she dressed, "I think that was Bu Bear. She had the same light spot by her right eye."

Arndis replied thoughtfully, "Perhaps. It has been several years since we have seen her and she would have a cub of her own by now. I wonder if she will come back to the farm?" She answered her own question, "We should be watchful, but I believe there is enough for her to eat in the woods so we needn't worry about our animals."

"She may come to show us her cub" said Freyja hopefully, "she was my favorite house bear."

Several times her grandfather had trapped and killed a mother bear and brought the cub home to be raised as a pet. The house bear was a popular pet among Freyja's people. The bear cub would spend its youth with the family being a wonderful playmate and cozy sleeping companion for the hearty children. When the bear got to be a juvenile, they would take it deep into the woods or it would wonder off to seek a mate. Often a young mother bear would come by with a new cub to show it off to her old human family. Freyja hoped that it had been Bu Bear they had seen today and that she would do just that.

Mother and daughter walked leisurely toward the farm carrying the clean clothing and chatting together. They talked of the house bears of the past and of Freyja's grandfather and grandmother. Stories of the past made them laugh and remember.

As they approached the house, they knew something was wrong. The door was open and they heard a screeching sound as if the table was being pushed across the floor. Things were being dropped or moved about loudly and forcefully and they heard some grunts. They put down their bundles and Arndis motioned Freyja to stay put while she crept up to the doorway. She was just about to peek into the house when, with a loud growl, Og stumbled out of the doorway.

He was shaking his hand and mumbling about hot pots, wives and the lack of mead. "No mead, no women, no food...," he droned. He sat down on the ground and Arndis crouched in front of him.

"Og, what is it?" she asked the sincere question.

"Helga is mad with me. She was mad when I would come here and now, she is mad when I am always at home. The Mead House has put me out, they say I cannot have more and now I am come to find no women here as well as no mead and my hand is hurting," Og told his sad story laboriously.

Arndis took his hand, "You have a burn. Come we will put it in water." She helped Og to his feet and into the house.

The cooking area was in disarray. Everything had been moved and explored. Crocks were uncovered and cloth bags opened. If there had been any mead, it truly would have been discovered. The pot which had been over the coals had been pulled out suggesting it might have been the cause of Og's burn. Arndis righted a bench and pushed Og down on it. "My house, what have you done?"

Og cast his eyes down with the look of a sad little boy and Arndis could no longer be angry. "Can, can I stay?" he stammered.

Arndis answered matter-of-factly, "We will eat and then to bed with the sun. Tomorrow we can make this mess right." She shook her head and got bowls of stew for the three of them while Freyja put away their washing. The food must have brought Og back to himself. He grabbed Arndis around the waist, "And now, we will to bed as you said."

"No," Arndis took his hands from her waist and surprised herself saying, "You will, to my bed by yourself and in the morning you will go. We share our house with you as with any guest."

Og looked at her, not understanding what she said. "I to your bed, but not you? Where will you go?"

"A mother can sleep with her child."

CHAPTER TEN

F reyja woke, warm near her mother, with a sweet feeling of childhood. When they rose, they discovered that Og was no longer there.

Several more weeks passed with the two women sharing the plentiful work about the farm and preparing things to take to market for trade. The abundant rabbits fed them and continued to supply pelts. These dried while staked to the southern wall of the house. They had no value at market, but made into items they might fetch a good trade.

Market day was quieter with most of the men gone, but it was still fun for people to gather together. They met at the three roads and then inevitably at the Mead House. The Old One was again receiving gifts for divination and the women were nodding at Freyja with good humor. She often caught them staring at her belly for signs of growth.

A trader from far away approached for a trade. He wore colorful clothing and beads in his black hair as Tahir had. Arndis pushed his coins aside and nodded at his bag of dried fruit.

"This would be a better trade for us," said Arndis kindly. He gave them far too many dried fruits in exchange for cheese and roots so that Freyja had some to trade for herself. She approached the mother of the twins and made a trade for the shawl she had been so desperately coveting. She put it on and twirled in front of her mother.

"It is beautiful on you," said Arndis.

"Yes," smiled Freyja. "I have wanted it for so long. I will wear it for Sven's return." Her face was fairly shining with happiness at the thought of their future meeting.

Freyja and Arndis went happily to the Mead House together after trading. Og stood up to shout his greeting, but Helga pulled him forcefully back down on the bench beside her. She made certain everyone knew, once again, of her disdain for the two women. Her sour face and glaring eyes left no doubt in anyone's mind.

Several of the boys, too young to be on a viking, motioned for Freyja and Arndis to join them. They moved to make spaces on the bench for the women. The boys speculated on how the expedition might be going for Sven and the men. The stories they made up were full of exciting discoveries of great hunting or fishing grounds. Each of them would interrupt the others to add incredible details. The boy sitting next to Freyja fantasized that perhaps they would even find new places for young couples to settle and touched her arm as he said it. He immediately blushed when he realized his over eagerness and stammered about leaving. He stood up awkwardly then fell with his face in Freyja's breasts when she reached out to steady him. There in her arms he just about fainted from embarrassment, but she hugged him and gently helped him back down on the bench. The others were ready to pounce with laughter at his mistake when she reached over to turn his head and plant a warm kiss upon his lips. The other boys watched with open mouths as the two women stood to leave. The lucky youth grinned from ear to ear.

Helga took this opportunity to stand up and lash out as the women passed her table. "How like your mother, you are Freyja," she said with a smirk. "You are ready to bed with all."

Arndis loudly took up Freyja's defense saying, "She was only showing a kindness to the young man, which I am glad to see you now doing with your own man. It has been a whole day since he has come to me seeking comfort." This was said loudly in passing so that all could hear and the two women continued out of the Mead House leaving Helga standing with her mouth open.

"But Mother you have not slept with Og for some time now. Why did you say that?" asked Freyja, outside once again. The fading sunlight made pale shadows of the trees at their feet.

"They will believe of me what they always have, but I do not want them to think of you that way. You have a different future and I am eager for it. And for the grandchildren to be mine," she smiled as she took Freyja's arm and patted her belly.

The women walked arm in arm, on the path home, talking and laughing. A cool breeze came off the ocean with the sunset and both glanced toward the sea. Freyja spoke the thought they both had. "I wonder of Sven and the voyage. I pray that all goes safely. I must begin to watch from our rocks for their return. I wonder what gifts he may bring me and if he will be ready to live under the same roof to begin our family. I so want the prophecy to unfold for us all, but ...," her voice trailed off with an edge of doubt to it.

"But what?" asked Arndis curtly. "This is meant to be Freyja; it can bring nothing but good for you, and Sven, and all of us." She smiled reassuringly.

Freyja began with a catch in her voice, "It is only that I am not sure of Sven, if he will even send the *fastnandi* to start the wedding negotiations."

Arndis was quick to end Freyja's worries, "Many relationships have begun from far less, Freyja. All will be fine. Think not of your doubts, but of the bright future." They had reached the farm. "And now let us enjoy the dried figs and dates along with our rabbit stew. They will be much tastier than the coins the trader wanted to give me."

Arndis and Freyja ate their *nattmal*, evening meal, in front of the fire, then said good night. Arndis to dream about Tahir, as the visiting trader had reminded her of the handsome man and his Moor culture. Freyja dreamt of Sven arriving with a boat full of treasurers and new alliances. He had many stories to tell all of their children yet to be born. He spoke to her of his love and the passion he would continue to share with her. Her dream felt so real that when she woke, she had a sense that the Old One and her mother were both right. All would work out and she and Sven would unite to have love and passion and bring the prophecy into being. She felt her grandmother's presence. *"We will see, Freyja. We will see."*

She lay in her bed, warm with her fur skins and touched herself as she imagined Sven would upon his return. Her hands slid down the length of her downy legs, feeling her strong and supple muscles. She touched her belly and her breasts thinking how she would enjoy feeling warm against his chest. They had not yet shared her bed, but she could feel how his body would fit next to hers. She imagined him on top of her and felt her legs open to his spirit. She played out their fantasy love making and felt as an opening blossom when she reached the height of her passion. She smiled, looking forward to Sven's timely return and said a prayer to *Frigga* for his safety.

Chapter Eleven

F reyja felt the days of Sven's viking nearing an end. She had not yet made the journey to the eastern peak to find the items the Old One had said she needed to offer to *Freyja* and *Freyr*. She wondered what man she should ask to join her. She knew few of the young men well enough to approach one with a task that would be done alone with her. Karle had sat by himself the last night at the Mead House, sullen, in a corner. He had not gone on the viking with the others as his family had all taken ill and he was needed on the farm. They had healed and he felt that his time had been wasted, but the Old One had insisted that he should stay behind.

Karle was a friend of Sven's and Freyja liked him well enough. She decided she would ask him next market day.

Market day was full of the chatter of women. Mothers were calling after their children and much gossip was being shared. Everyone's gardens were producing well so the trading was good natured without harsh negotiations. Freyja and Arndis brought radishes, rabbit skins, and new potatoes. There was not much that they really needed, but the twins' family had honeycombs and Arndis traded for these treats.

Freyja looked down the row of women along the road and found Karle among his family. He was on one knee, watching his two younger brothers play a game with stones. "Karle," Freyja called out. "What would you say to an adventure?"

Karle frowned at her. "I have no adventures this season." He motioned with his head toward his parents.

His mother walked up behind him and patted him on the back. "You did your duty for your kin," she said warmly. "Karle did not go with the others, to care for his family. He is a fine warrior."

"I have heard such," Freyja replied with a smile. "I must ask if your family can spare him to help me with my search for items to offer to the twin gods of fertility and prosperity."

Karle's father stepped up to join the conversation. "We are pleased to help insure the good favor of *Freyr* and *Freyja*. We, like all, hope for good crops and increase in our animals and our own numbers." He smiled as he patted his wife's round belly.

Her round face beamed back at him. "Karle can help you gather in the woods today or any other time." She touched Karle's shoulder and he shrugged it off as he stood up and stepped away, his eyes downcast.

"The Old One has told me that I must journey above the tree line on the rocky peak *Grjot Fell* to seek such things." Freyja pointed with her chin at the formidable mountain rising to the east. "She says I must not go to our known woods and must take a man with me. I had hoped Karle might want to come with me." She looked at Karle hopefully, but he was looking down at his feet.

"Karle is your man, for this," bellowed Karle's father with a large grin. His mother nodded enthusiastically while the little brothers crowded around her skirts. "He will be ready when you are going. The farm is on your way."

"I will give you bread and milk to start your journey. I also have salted fish which travels well. All this I will send with you," said Karle's mother.

It seemed to Freyja that Karle's parents were very eager for him to make the journey or at least to leave the farm. "How is it with you, Karle?" Freyja asked. "Will you come with me to seek the things for my offerings?"

Karle finally looked up and into Freyja's eyes. "Yes. As Sven's friend and kin, I will help you. To have even a small adventure, as you say, will be good," said Karle. He kicked at a stone and a small smile appeared on his lips. He nodded, "Come to the farm and I will go with you."

"This is well, Karle. I am glad for your help. I will return in a few days," Freyja nodded. She smiled and waved her goodbyes to the family then walked toward the Mead House where she thought she might find her mother.

Freyja bumped her leg into the first table inside the room as her eyes adjusted to the lack of light. "Freyja, join your mother and us. We are sharing some honeycomb," said one of the old brothers.

"Greetings, Daughter. We taste the honey from the comb and the honey made into mead. Sit and tell me of your day." Arndis seemed in a good mood and was comfortable among her old friends.

"Karle has said that he will go with me and his mother will send bread and milk. I will go in a few days' time," Freyja shared eagerly. She saw the expectant faces of the old brothers and explained. "The Old One sends me to *Grjot Fell* the rocky peak, above the tree line, to gather offerings for the gods."

The old men nodded solemnly. "We know the peak, but not well. It will be good to fill your water skins at the waterfall, before you begin the climb," spoke one brother. "We stop there many times after a hunt for good water. We are too old for the path up to the peak." A worried look passed between the brothers and the speaker continued, "It would be well to give offering to the *land vaettir* on your journey, as well. The mountain spirits are sometimes tricky."

Arndis frowned and looked at Freyja from the corner of her eye. Freyja caught the mood and spoke hurriedly, "Perhaps that is why the Old One said that I should bring a man with me. Karle knows his sword and will surely aid me. I will bring good cheese and mead for the *vaettir,* in any case." She smiled and patted her mother's hand.

The subject of talk soon changed and then Arndis and Freyja began their walk to the farm. "So, you will take Karle to the rocky peak with you?" Arndis spoke. Freyja nodded, yes. "I know his family and he will do as you ask, if it will please the gods. As for you... I ask that you keep your eyes and ears open. Listen to the gods and look for signs. It may be a hard journey, but the Old One has set you on it."

They walked the rest of the way home in silence.

CHAPTER TWELVE

In two days, Freyja had gathered what she needed for her journey. She packed her water skin, her knife, a flint, cheese, mead, and dried rabbit meat. She bundled her things in her winter cloak as her mother had said that nights above the tree line could be cold. "We will take the horse to the family of Karle to rest your legs and back before you begin," said Arndis in her "no arguing" voice. She walked alongside the horse and chatted about the forest and what berries might be in abundance at the base of the rocky peak. "You may find berries near the waterfall. It could make for a pleasant beginning of your climb. You should be sure to dedicate some to the *vaettir* of the place as well."

"Yes, mother. I have cheese and mead for them as well. It is good to seek what help I might." She smiled at her mother, knowing that this would make her happy. Having her mother worry about her was a new idea. She had always been healthy and strong and the prophecy protected her in many ways. She pushed any thoughts of doubt away as they sighted the family farm and heard a noisy greeting from the young brothers.

"Freyja is here," they yelled together and ran to greet Freyja and Arndis. They walked with them along the path to the farmhouse, pointing out their chickens, goats, sheep, and cattle. It was a busy farm with a half a dozen servants working with Karle's parents. The smell of fresh bread tickled their noses when Karle's mother opened the door. She waddled down the steps to greet them.

"Greetings Arndis and Freyja. You are welcome. I have bread and milk for you and Karle will bring a goat. She can be milked and maybe keep you warm at night," she giggled. She handed a cloth wrapped disk of bread and a skin filled with milk to Freyja.

Karle clomped down the steps in a hurry, "We should go. We do not know what the day holds." He had a bundle on his back and went to get a goat from his father.

Freyja now had her bundle on her back and a large walking stick in hand. "Thank you for your gifts. We will return when we have found what the Old One has asked for." She hugged her mother goodbye and heard the two women begin talking as she turned her back to the farm. She saw Karle's father clap him on the shoulders and laugh heartily. Then Karle hurried to catch up with her, leading the goat. He glared at Freyja.

"You said you would be going," Freyja responded with her own glare. Then she laughed, "Thank you for coming. I know your family pledged for you, and not yourself."

"I have nothing other to do," replied Karle. "At least I can be away from them for a time." Karle shook his head. "There is only work on the farm. I have missed much, but will hear great stories when Sven and the others return." His face looked a combination of anger and sadness.

"Well, perhaps our journey will be one to tell tales of. We have a mission from the Old One and travel to a place unknown to both of us. I believe the gods will favor us." Freyja spoke a bit too cheerfully.

Karle just shrugged and walked more slowly, letting the goat nibble as it wanted. They walked toward the meeting of the three roads, then left the road and headed east. Walking in the shade of the rocky peak was comfortable until *Sol* reached the summit of her chariot ride and they began to feel warm from the rays of the sun. As they walked, Freyja's load began to feel heavy and the ties looped over her shoulders began to dig into her muscles. She stopped under the shade of a tree and searched for her water skin. "I will stop and take water," Freyja spoke to Karle then realized he was behind her. He caught up to her, nodded silently and continued walking. The goat trailed behind him on its rope.

Freyja drank and in some time, caught up with Karle who was walking slowly with the goat. The sound of a waterfall greeted their ears and they smiled at one another. "I will take water at the waterfall," yelled Karle over his shoulder as he ran ahead. The goat must have smelled the water because she too ran.

A thicket surrounded the opening to the glade with the pool and waterfall. They walked through an opening into the secluded tiny meadow.

There were well-worn banks along the edge of the pool, at the base of the waterfall, where people must come to collect water. Freyja put down her bundle and knelt gladly in the shade to fill her waterskin. The water was cold and she splashed some on her face and neck to refresh herself. "This is welcome," she said to Karle. Karle lay on his belly with his lips to the pool. He slurped loudly and then sighed with satisfaction as he rolled over on his back to cross his legs at his ankles. He had let the goat go and she was drinking. The goat then proceeded to happily graze the thick undergrowth as the pair of travelers rested.

"I will look before we begin climbing to the peak," Freyja said. She settled her bundle on the ground and put her arm through the cord of her waterskin to sling it over her shoulder. Freyja soon found berries and marked their location so she could gather some on her return to the waterfall. She found amber dotted on a tree and dug some out with her knife. It was good enough for her, but she had been instructed to find some for the goddess on the mountain. As she peered through the thick forest up the hill to the top of the peak, she could see that the trees began to get thinner. Where the tree line ended it revealed only rock nearer the top. The name *Grjot Fell*, or rocky peak, was the description used by everyone and it was well named.

Freyja's soft boots felt comfortable on the loam of the forest floor and she found herself back at the berry patch without any trouble. She gathered several handfuls for her pouch and also found mushrooms good for eating. When she came back to the clearing of the waterfall, Karle appeared to be asleep. The goat wandered, dragging the rope and seemed unconcerned. Freyja sat beside him and shook his shoulder. "I have found berries to share," she said holding out a handful. "We can eat these before we go." Karle reached over and greedily took most of the handful. Knowing that she had a second handful, she retrieved them from her pouch. When Karle had finished his berries, he reached over to take more berries from Freyja's hand. "Karle, these were for us two. You have eaten many." Karle only shrugged and lay down again, on his side. He drew slowly in the dirt with a stick.

In a few moments he stretched and yawned. "We will stay here, for the night. I will milk the goat and my mother has sent bread. Can you make a fire?"

Freyja knitted her brow, "Karle, we are to find offerings for the gods. We have more time until darkness. We should walk up the peak some more."

"Yes Freyja, you have said it, we have time so let us go slowly and enjoy the journey," he raised his eyebrows.

Freyja did not argue, but started a small fire. Karle milked the goat into a bowl he had brought and Freyja got out the loaf of bread from Karle's mother. "We also have cheese, yes?" asked Karle.

"Tonight, we have milk and bread, with our berries and mushrooms. I save cheese for offerings to the land spirits," replied Freyja testily. She broke off bread for both of them and handed Karle his piece along with exactly half of the mushrooms. He drank milk from the bowl and passed it to Freyja. "Thank you for the milk, Karle," she said pointedly.

Although it was just beginning to get cool, Karle moved in front of the fire. After he finished eating, he spread out next to the fire. When Freyja raised her eyebrow with the question, he patted the space next to him. "There is room for you right here. We will be most warm side by side," Karle smiled his most pleasing smile.

"Karle, you know I wait for Sven," Freyja said patiently, but rolled her eyes. She made a place for herself with just her feet near the fire.

Karle was asleep as soon as the sun set. Freyja tended the fire. The goat began to bleat and skitter about on the end of its rope. Karle had tied it to a tree but it could not be seen in the dark. Freyja stumbled her way to the animal. She had pulled her small knife and was ready to call on Karle.

There seemed nothing to cause the animal worry, so Freyja tied it closer to them and returned to the fire. She sat for a while thinking about her journey and the "man she may not need" as she recalled the Old One saying. She unwrapped the cheese and broke a piece off along with a piece of bread. She took these to a flat rock near the back side of the fire that looked as it had been used for offerings before. "Hail the gods. Hail the *vaettir*. I bring you cheese and bread from our homes. We hope that you will find favor with us as we journey to find offerings for gods who came from the *Vanir* to join the *Aesir*. We offer this food to you, the *vaettir*, in hopes that it will please you and you will not mind our activity on your mountain." She placed the food on the rock. "I bring you mead. May its sweet flavor please you and give you sustenance. Please accept my offerings," Freyja poured some mead into a bowl like hollow hewn into the rock.

She sat for some time, listening to the quiet of the dark night. The sound of the fire soothed her and she lay down to sleep.

When she awoke it was first light. She realized that she was warm. She was on her cloak, sleeping on her side, and her back was perfectly warm. Karle had rearranged himself to curl around her back. His arm was across her hips. Freyja ducked her chin, then rocked her head back so that she hit against Karle's forehead. "By the gods!" Karle yelped. "I am awake now."

"I did not try to wake you. I try again to tell you that I wait for Sven. I do not want to sleep near you." Freyja lifted his hand to remove it from her hips.

Karle grabbed her wrist and pulled her on her back as he rose to his knees. He looked down on her, "It is only my friendship with Sven that keeps you safe. I could abandon you to whatever fate the rocky peak holds for you." He let go of her and stood.

Freyja glared at him while rubbing her wrist. The words of the Old One came back to her, *"take a man that you may not need"*. She began to gather her things.

Freyja clenched her jaw and silently filled her water skin. "I go to gather some berries and begin the climb.," she said tersely. She returned to the bushes she had found the day before. She heard Karle muttering as he began to gather his things.

Freyja soon heard him crashing through the brush. He emerged, pulling the goat behind him, while chewing something. Perhaps he had found more mushrooms, though they must be very chewy. She handed Karle some berries which he quickly downed. He immediately turned to the bushes to eat more, the goat joining him.

"We leave the forest soon. The way is steep and rocky so I will walk in a pattern up the hill much like the roads down the fjords," Freyja said.

"Let us walk then," said Karle rolling his eyes.

Freyja began walking to the right and diagonally up the hill. When the slope changed, she walked to the left and diagonally up. "Our day will be long, walking like this," yelled Karle up to her.

"We can rest beneath that lone tree," Freyja pointed to a singular pine tree providing a large patch of shade. She focused her attention on that goal even with Karle's constant whining.

"It grows hot without shade. The goat seems to tire," Karle remarked.

"We will rest soon, Karle. We can take water in the shade. It is not much farther," Freyja reassured him. She continued their upward climb as the sun also climbed. They would just make it to the tree to enjoy some shade before the sun reached its zenith.

Freyja got to the base of the tree and sat gratefully in the shade. She put down her bundle and reached for her waterskin. The water was a true blessing from the gods. Karle reached the tree moments behind her and began gulping water from his own skin. The goat came to him bleating pitifully as if she wanted water as well. He kicked her away.

Freyja held out her hand to the goat and poured some water into her palm. The goat licked her hand and she giggled. "There is little for the goat to eat here. I hope we can find the things that I need quickly so that she does not hunger," Freyja mused. The goat went to the base of the tree and began to nibble on moss and bark. It soon stood on its hind legs to reach some needles.

"She eats now," Karle shrugged. "I will milk her so we can have the milk while we rest."

Freyja was anxious to climb, but saw that the goat was uncomfortable and needed to be milked. She scanned the mountainside and noted the changes they would experience on their climb to the top. "Up further there is no more green and no trees. We may find shade and protection next to boulders. I am glad now that my mother said to bring my warm cloak." Freyja spoke while she looked uphill.

Karle had filled his bowl with goat's milk and seemed to be enjoying it as he sat with his back against the tree. "Come Freyja, the milk is good. You should drink while I gather fire wood." He handed her the bowl and went about gathering wood.

Freyja frowned after him. "We have only climbed half the day, Karle. We can get much nearer the top if we keep going," Freyja urged him.

"You say this is the last tree for shelter and may be the last place for wood. We can rest well here and begin fresh tomorrow." Karle spoke not looking at her, but appeared to be engrossed in his work. "If I gather too much, we will use it on our way back down."

Freyja made an angry face, but bit her tongue. She had this help and should appreciate it, but she was driven. She sat in the growing shade on the east side of the tree and sharpened her knife. She took off her boots and dried and aired her feet in the sunshine. She cleaned her fingernails with her sharpened knife then retied her boots. She wondered at Karle's hesitation. Was he fearful of the task or was he hoping to stay longer from his farm?

As the shadow of their lone tree lengthened, Karle made a campfire. He had gathered wood enough for several days. He smiled at the pile then lit a spark to ignite the fire. Freyja had to admit that it was well made and it felt good as the afternoon was cooling. "We should be drinking and singing this night," Karle said. "Have you mead still?" he asked.

"I have, for the land *vaettir*," replied Freyja. "I will leave an offering for them now so that we will earn their favor and protection." She took the skin of mead and broke off a piece of cheese, leaving its bag under the tree. Down the hill aways she found a flat boulder with some broken bits on top. Using the butt of her knife she broke more of these pieces and scooped them out to create a hollow. "Hail, the land *vaettir*. We offer you of our mead and cheese in hopes that you will find our presence on your mountain acceptable. Grant us safe passage on our journey." She poured mead into the hollow and left the piece of cheese. She sat watching the sun set and waited to see if she was given any message. In the half-light she stumbled back up to the fire.

Karle had spread his cloak on the ground. His feet were near the fire and his head rested on his folded hands. He was chewing on a small twig and seemed to be picking at his teeth. Freyja's stomach rumbled as she kicked some stones away to make a smooth place for herself to lie down. She thought of the dried rabbit she carried and the salted fish in Karle's bundle, but knew they should be saved. They would have fresh goat's milk in the morning anyway. She made herself comfortable wrapped in her cloak, near the fire and fell asleep.

Freyja woke to the sound of quiet singing. It sounded like Karle, but she must have been dreaming. There seemed to be only a few coals left of their fire and the temperature had dropped. She reached to the wood pile and put another branch on the fire. It caught quickly and then the light faded to coals again. Maybe if she added more wood, she could see Karle by the light. She put another branch on the fire and the same thing happened. It was as if the fire only wanted to be small coals. She sat up and pulled her cloak tightly around her as she inched closer to the fire. The wind began to howl almost like voices, but she knew that could not be.

She dozed, off and on, until the sky began to lighten. Freyja opened her eyes and shook her head, remembering back to the cold night. Her back was now being warmed by the rising sun which felt glorious. A small piece of golden light from *Sol* was growing very slowly from the center of her back. She stretched her neck trying to work the kinks out then leaned forward and blew on the embers to get the fire going. It sprang to life easily as Freyja shook her head remembering the night. Another branch was added as she looked around for Karle. Where was he?

Freyja stood up slowly, easing the stiffness out of her legs. She looked all around for Karle until her eyes rested on a pile near the boulder where she had left her offerings to the land *vaettir*. "Karle," she yelled. "Oh *Odin*, are you well?" She raced down the hill slipping several times on loose rocks and grabbed at Karle's cloak.

"Hey, you grab at my ankles like *Skadi*, the giantess, searching for *Balder's* feet, to marry him. Though my ankles must be as fair as a god, I thought you wait for Sven," Karle almost growled as he sat up squinting in the sun. Freyja's mead skin lay on the ground and she picked it up to find it empty. The cheese, which she had left on the boulder, was gone.

"Karle," Freyja sent daggers from her narrowed eyes. "You have called misfortune on us." She held up the mead skin and pointed to the bare rock.

"So, the land *vaettir* hunger, just like us," Karle shrugged nonchalantly as he stood and brushed off his clothing.

"I worry now of their anger. I have given to them and you have taken from them. They will feel the need for revenge.

All night the fire would not burn. Your actions of disrespect will not be ignored."

"Then let us get on with your quest and leave this place soon," Karle replied with a sour look. "I will milk the goat. What else do you have for us to eat?"

Freyja shook her head with exasperation. "I will eat the dried rabbit from my trapping and will share with the *vaettir*. You have salted fish from you mother and should do so as well."

Karle rolled his eyes at her and shuffled up the hill to where the goat was nibbling on the tree. He milked the goat and began to drink loudly from his bowl. "Here, Freyja. I have saved some milk for you." He held out the bowl for her to take.

"I would have you leave mine for the land *vaettir*," Freyja said coldly.

Karle looked at her defiantly. "If you do not want it, I will drink it gladly." He drank and then offered the bowl to the goat. She licked it happily then began to chew on it until Karle took it away.

Freyja had gathered her bundle and kicked out the fire as Karle drank. She went down to the boulder with some rabbit meat in her hand. She placed it reverently on the rough surface. "I ask you, land *vaettir*, to forgive Karle and grant us permission to travel unharmed upon your mountain," Freyja whispered. She turned to take one step up the hill. A large raven appeared from nowhere. Its shadow covered the boulder as it snatched the rabbit meat in its beak. It dove at Freyja so that she ducked and covered her head with her arms. She yelled unconsciously with surprise as she watched it fly toward the tree. Another met it on the top of the tree. "Even *Odin* does not approve of what you do, Karle. He sends his ravens, *Hugin* and *Munin*. They will tell him what they see."

Freyja walked with purpose and anger back to the tree and began the steep climb uphill toward the summit. She walked in the same pattern up the hill, slowly, carefully. Her anger made her want to walk more quickly, but she knew the loose rocks could spell disaster if she slipped or started several rocks falling down the hill. She could hear Karle coming behind her, but did not look around. They walked in silence as the sun climbed.

When the sun was at its highest Freyja stopped to drink from her water skin. She could hear Karle panting as he climbed straight up the hill near her. "We will save time if we travel straight," Karle yelled. He was pulling the poor goat behind him as he passed her. He made it about half the distance to the top in a short time while Freyja continued walking in her pattern. He turned to look down the hill at Freyja. "You see, I help your journey greatly." He smiled and waved his hand toward the summit. "I will be at the top waiting for you soon." He took a few forceful steps for emphasis and the mountain came alive.

Several stones came loose under his feet and he slid down hill, still standing upright. He shrugged and smiled at Freyja seeming not to be worried. As he slid, more stones from above came loose to follow after him. In slow motion he went down on one knee and the dust rose. In seconds

Freyja could no longer see him. A cloud of dust filled the air and the sound was like thunder.

As it quieted and the dust settled Freyja looked for Karle. He was sitting with his feet under a pile of stones, holding a rope in his hand. The goat was nowhere to be seen. "My foot," he yelled in pain.

"Stay still, I will come to you," Freyja called to him. She started slowly down the hill making a new pattern as her old path was beneath stones now. She glanced periodically to watch Karle pull rocks away from his feet. Once both feet were out, she could see some blood on one of his boots. "Karle, are you broken?" she called.

"I do not think so," Karle yelled back. He stood slowly and tried to walk, but his right foot would not bear his weight. "I can no longer climb the rocky peak, Freyja. You must continue without me. I will rest under the tree." He pointed to their fire and the shade of the tree below. He began to inch his way down toward his resting spot, scooting along the rocks like a spider.

Freyja felt tears of frustration sting her eyes. Perhaps she should have taken this journey alone, but the Old One had said to take a man, that she may not need. For what purpose? "Be well, Karle," Freyja called, with a big breath, then she continued her climb.

Chapter Thirteen

Freyja climbed. Back and forth she walked along the face of the rocky peak. She could see the top getting imperceptibly closer. She knew the top was her goal, but tried not to think about it. She felt discouraged. Although Karle had proved to be useless, he had been a companion. She could have used someone to talk to or at least to take her mind off the quest that now seemed impossible. Where was she to find amber or a boar, as commanded on the barren landscape of *Grjot Fell* ahead?

The sweat poured off her as she faced the sun. The rocks still radiated heat as the sun moved behind her. She stopped often to adjust her bundle and ease her shoulders. She forced herself to swallow, rather than spit, as she knew her water skin was getting light. When she neared the top a cooling breeze greeted her. She wanted to strip down and bathe in its coolness, but the summit was near enough to see. Freyja dragged herself up the last of the climb and reached the peak just in time to watch the sunset.

She slumped down on her haunches with relief. "Hail, the gods and thank you. I have reached the top of *Grjot Fell*." The expanse before her was breathtaking. The tiny ribbons of creeks, surrounded by trees, flowed to their *fjord*. She could see smoke rising from the village cook fires. The sun was touching the ocean and she watched for the green flash, the moment after the sun set upon the water, that she knew would follow soon.

Flash. The green light filled her heart with wonder and she sighed deeply. She looked down the hill to see firelight blaze up near the lone tree. Karle must have been able to light the fire. She began to search for wood to make a fire of her own. It would signal to Karle that she too was alright.

Freyja unloaded her bundle and created a fire ring of the many rocks. There was dried moss hiding under a nearby boulder that she could use as fire starter. She began to search for wood. There were several tree stumps, seemingly very old. She pried a few bits of bark from their bases and gnarled exposed roots. She widened her search in a larger circle and was able to find branches enough for a night fire. Her pile of firewood grew as the wind picked up.

A bitter cold began to settle on the rocky peak and Freyja decided to move her firepit in front of a large boulder and use it as a windbreak. She left space for her to sleep between the fire and the boulder in hopes that the rock would reflect the heat of the fire. She got out her flint and knelt to light the moss and small bits of bark. A spark. It sputtered and died.

She felt around in her bundle to see what she might have. A bit of cheese, dried rabbit meat, an empty skin of mead. She thought about the offerings to the land *vaettir* of this place. Karle had surely brought their anger by eating of the offering meant for them. The picture of him joining her at the berry bushes before their climb entered her mind. He had been chewing. Had he eaten the first offering she had left at the waterfall as well? Her mouth fell open with the realization. He had caused the rockslide by his stupidity as well as his theft of what was not meant for him. She gritted her teeth and shook her head.

Her shoulders began to shake with anger and the cold. She wrapped herself in her cloak and approached the top of the boulder. "Hail the land *vaettir*. I offer you gifts from my heart in hopes that you will not see me as a threat. I come seeking amber and a boar as gifts to *Freyr* and *Freyja*. I will find them and then leave you in peace." She placed a piece of cheese and rabbit meat on the rock's surface and held the mead skin over the top. She upended it and a small trickle of mead caressed the rock. She began to wring the skin and more mead flowed out. This was now a small, but proper offering. "Hail the land *vaettir*."

Freyja turned back to her fire and gathered the moss and bark in her hands. She had an inspiration and put it down. She untied one boot and pulled at the squirrel skin lining. Once she had a bit of fur, she added it to her fire starter. She struck her flint and a spark landed in the little nest. She gently cupped the little nest in her hands and blew on the spark until a flame started. That done, she placed the flaming ball at the base of her fire.

She slowly fed the fire, then settled with her back against the boulder. Her eyes began to close and she was engulfed by exhaustion. She must have dozed for a while then woke to lay herself down. The boulder was indeed a bit warm and she put her back against it as she curled up with her cloak over her. She woke several times in the night and fed the fire to keep it going. The night was cold, but she was comfortable enough.

She slept long after sunrise, in the shade of the boulder. Her fire was down to coals and she added a branch before she stood up into the warm sunlight. She stood to stretch and noticed a wet spot at the base of the boulder. Moisture must have dripped off the stone in the night to make a small pool beneath one side. She knelt down with the empty mead skin and coaxed some water into its throat. It was not bad tasting, flavored with mead, and she was refreshed. She heaved a grateful sigh, relieved to know that she would not die of thirst. Now to begin her quest on the rocky peak.

Freyja banked the coals of her fire and began to explore. She found much petrified wood, but knew it would be of no use. An armload of bark was taken back to her fire after a long search. The shadows of birds passed over the rough ground during the day, but she saw no other signs of life. The rocks would make it hard to track animals even if there were any. After midday she sat on the east side of the boulder in the shade and chewed on a piece of dried rabbit meat. She chewed slowly, allowing her saliva to soften the meat. She could feel the gift of strength that it gave her. What was she to do? Had the Old One sent her on a fool's errand?

The gift of amber was to be given to the goddess *Freyja*, for whom she was named. The gift of a boar would be given to the goddess' twin brother *Freyr*. Together they ensured the fertility and prosperity of animals and people. These offerings would surely help her and Sven fulfill the village prophecy. They would be fertile and children would be born. Thus, would the prosperity foretold be revealed to their people. Tears came to her eyes as she doubted this journey, but she knew she must continue her search. She fell asleep against the rock and drifted down into the earth she sat upon.

She dreamt of the dwarfs making the necklace, *Brisingamen,* so highly prized by the goddess *Freyja*. They worked deep in the caverns of the earth below. Their fires blazed hot and their hammers rang as they fashioned the necklace of gold and amber. Freyja leaned back against the cave wall, watching them as they each watched her lustfully. She knew she would have to give them each a night of desires in exchange for the necklace. She found herself removing her overdress, then the rest of her clothing and laying back on a bed that suddenly appeared. One of the dwarfs came to her and began fondling her breasts. He was ugly and his hands were rough.

Her dream changed and she found herself fighting with a very large bird over a small boar. Her hands were covered in blood and scratches. She tried to pry the bird's talons open to release the boar as it pecked at her. She knew the boar would still die after she freed it, but felt that she must have it. She found a rabbit and threw it as far as she could, hoping that the bird would chase it. The bird opened its talons and pecked her right arm as an angry farewell. Freyja held the little boar in her arms as it closed its eyes and took its last breath.

Freyja woke groggily, her eyes not focusing, not knowing where she was. The shadow of the boulder was very long and the wind was picking up. She stood shakily, and held on to the boulder as she walked around it. She added wood and blew on the coals until the fire blazed up. She squinted down the hill, but did not see a fire near the tree. She thought of Karle, but did not worry. His fate was in the hands of the gods and perhaps the land *vaettir*, as well. A smirk appeared on her mouth. She did not wish him ill, but any problems he encountered would be brought on by his own actions.

She sat next to the fire, brooding. This day had been wasted. She had found only a bit of firewood. Night would come soon and be long. With nothing else to do, she sharpened her knife and put it back at her belt. The sun set. The wind rose. Freyja decided to go over the peak to the east that she had not explored. She might find firewood. In the waning light her foot bumped against a pile of something. Perhaps it was a carcass. She went back to the fire to make a torch.

Torch in hand, she returned to the pile. It was the skeleton of a warrior wrapped in a tattered disintegrating cloak. A shield and sword lay beside it. As she held her torch high, a glint of gold was reflected from a grand necklace. Heavy gold, inlaid with amber. The tears of the goddess

Freyja. Freyja could barely contain her excitement. She put her torch in a cleft between two boulders and reached for the necklace.

As Freyja reached her hand to lift the necklace the empty eye sockets began to come alive. Ice blue eyes stared into hers and the eyelids narrowed. The skull was covered with pale translucent skin and a woman's face appeared. The specter glared at her while a bony hand clasped around her wrist. The hand grew in strength as it fleshed out. "I have waited alone on Grjot Fell between *Midgard* and *Valhalla*. I will defend my honor and what is mine," growled the undead shield-maiden. Lips were now covering her teeth and she pulled on Freyja to sit up. She clutched her side, where her breast plate was pierced, with her free hand. "You may not steal from me," she roared.

The wight pushed Freyja to the ground and reached for her sword. She held the rust and moss-covered weapon in both hands poised over Freyja. "Hold," Freyja called out loudly. She wrapped both her arms across the back of her neck. "I am Freyja and would have only taken what a dead maiden would no longer need."

The shield-maiden lowered her sword and leaned on it. She bent at the waist, favoring her wounded side. "The goddess?" she gasped. "Why do you pretend to be a stupid village girl?"

"I am named for the goddess Freyja and am from the village to the west of *Grjot Fell*," Freyja said as she rose to one knee. "I come in search of offerings for *Freyja* and *Freyr*. I must find amber and your necklace has such."

"I will fight you for it," the shield-maiden hissed through gritted teeth that were surrounded by puckered flesh.

"I cannot fight you, for you must be a wight and are already dead. My knife would not hurt you as you live by the power of some magic," Freyja said in desperation.

"Will you trade for it?" asked the shield-maiden. "You must have something of value."

"No. Only what you see," answered Freyja. She squeezed her eyes shut. Her journey was now truly cursed and she might die at the hands of this ghost.

"You can share tales with me of the world as it is now. I know nothing of what has happened since we were defeated in battle and I came to rest on *Grjot Fell*. Tell me of this land," the shield-maiden pleaded. "After your words, I will have tasks for you. Then we may call it a trade." The bony woman sank to the ground. She rested her sword on the ground and watched Freyja with interest.

Freyja began to tell her of her village and what lay west of the mountain. She spoke of the farming and trading that they did. "More raids are returning with wealth than ever before. Unusual things and people come to us now," Freyja spoke and the woman listened.

"What of the east side of the mountain? That is where we fought and all died there, but me. I hid as I listened to their taunts and the lewd talk of what would be done with me after my capture. It took me all the dark hours to climb to the peak so quietly that I would not be heard. In the morning I could barely hear them yelling and looking for me. It made me smile."

"Your breast plate was pierced?" Freyja asked while pointing to it.

"Yes. It is what caused my death. A spear, just as if I were a cornered boar pinned between the rocks. I could not fight honorably and was cursed for it. I am denied *Valhalla* and must roam this desolate peak forever."

Freyja told her what she knew of the east side of the rocky peak, *Grjot Fell,* which was only some second-hand stories from visitors to the Mead House. "Do your people know of your fate. Shall I tell the tale of your death?"

"No," the woman replied angrily. "I do not want any to know of my shame. Sneaking off to hide in the night. I should have died with my comrades and received a death of honor. My family is of *Odin* and the knowledge would bring them dishonor."

There was silence for a long time. "My words have satisfied you? I wish I had more to tell you, but I would like to trade for your necklace," Freyja said timidly. Who was to know how this ghost would react?

"I have a task for trade. You must fight and kill me. Then you must bury me with my sword so that I will finally rest and join my brothers and sisters in *Valhalla.*"

Freyja shook her head with her mouth open, "You are already dead. How can I kill you?"

"The magic you have spoken of has brought me to life, from your touch, on this dark night. In the morning I will be only a skeleton again, but each night I will rise again as a wight, one undead. If I can have an honorable death and be buried properly the *Valkyries* will carry me to *Valhalla,*" the woman smiled wistfully. Freyja could catch a glimpse of the humanity that had once embodied this shield-maiden.

"I have only my small knife," Freyja spoke quietly, "but I will do as you ask."

The woman looked gratefully at Freyja. "I will give you my *seax*," she said and pulled it out from behind her belt. "You may keep it and the necklace after you bury me with my sword. Your word bonds you to this agreement." She handed Freyja the long knife.

The knife was as rusted as the sword, but Freyja took it solemnly, with both hands outstretched. She removed her cloak in the cold wind and widened her stance, poised to fight. She tried to recall all the sparring she had seen between the men of the village.

The woman shape over the skeleton also removed her cloak. It broke into pieces as it hit the ground. She used two hands to swing her sword at Freyja. Freyja danced carefully back over the many loose stones. Dust puffed up under her feet, but was barely visible in the torch light. Freyja tried to get close enough to use the short sword, but the woman was a good defensive swordsman. Sweat was beginning to bead up on Freyja's lip and she licked off the salty moisture.

The woman lunged at Freyja causing Freyja to duck and stumble. She went down on one knee, receiving a bloody gash, but recovered quickly. She had no idea what being killed by a wight could do to her, and she did not want to find out. In a panic she flailed, trying to get her long knife close to the woman. The woman attacked with several more lunges, narrowly missing Freyja's midsection. She spun and bobbed wildly staying out of reach.

Freyja remembered her visions with the goddess and calmed her mind and her breath. She thought of the brief lesson that Tahir had shown her and took a defensive stance. This woman, immortal as she was, had no different body areas than herself. She could strike a wounding blow if she only concentrated.

In a foolish move, Freyja opened her stance which invited the woman's sword, but was able to block it with the *seax*. The woman sent her sword again at Freyja and the flat of the blade managed to hit the girl as Freyja spun in the opposite direction narrowly missing the slice of the blade. Freyja continued to spin and came behind to plunge the *seax* into the ghost's back. Freyja pulled out the long knife easily. It was covered in a glowing substance.

The ghost woman gasped then smiled. "You have pierced me. I feel the pain," she shouted gleefully. She turned to face Freyja with one hand to her back. With the other hand she leaned on her sword.

Freyja faced her and she knew that she must continue with respect. This woman had lived the life of a warrior and deserved the same death and afterlife of honor. Freyja stepped forward and the woman raised her sword with both hands and much effort. Freyja stepped in close allowing the woman's sword to graze her upper arm. The rusted steel left several rows of ragged cuts. She grabbed the woman's shoulder with her free hand, supporting her as she bent her back, then plunged the *seax* under the bottom of the chest plate up into her heart.

The shield-maiden dropped her sword and let Freyja take her weight. Freyja gently guided her down to the ground. With her arms on Freyja's shoulders, she looked into her eyes. "You have acted with honor as the name of your goddess. I gift you my necklace and my *seax* according to our trade. You must bury me with my sword and tell no one of my fortune. Now finish it." Freyja nodded in agreement, though she could not speak.

In a final tribute, Freyja took the sword in both of her hands. With widened feet she raised the old sword high over her head and brought it down across the specter's neck. The head separated from the body of the skeleton and the necklace fell to the ground in between.

Freyja looked down on what seemed only to be a skeleton now and felt a sadness creep over her. She had formed an unusual friendship with this ghost and was now saying goodbye. She had been a knowledgeable adversary in their fight and Freyja admired her skill. A warrior such as she, could have been a worthy mentor to learn from. Freyja wondered about knowing someone like her. It would be a good thing to talk of battle with a friend.

Suddenly, the horizon to the north filled with swirls of gold, green, and blue. The swirls grew closer with the sound of thundering hoofs. Freyja could now see that the swirls were the forelegs of many horses riding toward them in the sky. On their backs rode maidens clothed in armor, some brandishing swords. It could be none other than the *Valkyries.* One of the shield-maidens landed and knelt beside what was now a skeleton and held out her hand. A shimmering hand reached up and a beautiful woman rose to greet her with an embrace. Together they climbed on the horse and then with a nod to Freyja, off they rode into the flaming night sky.

Freyja cleared away stones from the surface of the ground to make a space large enough for a burial. She used the sword to pry stones up and pulled more from the ground. With her own knife she hacked at the hard earth and lifted dirt out with the battered old shield. The wind howled around her, but she felt warm from the exertion. Her hair whipped her shoulders and she wiped hairs from her face with the back of her hand. She paused, raising her head and realized that her torch had gone out, but there was still plenty of light to work with. The lights of the *Valkyries'* ride continued to fill the sky.

When the sun rose, Freyja had dug a decent burial space. She lay the tattered bits of cloak on the bottom and then placed the skeleton reverently together. On top of the torso, she placed the chest plate followed by the shield placed lower down the body. The arms were brought up on the chest so that it looked as if the shield-maiden's hands held the sword. Freyja placed stones so that the bones would stay in position, reverent and fit for a warrior. "You are now buried in honor," Freyja spoke aloud as she moved earth to cover the skeleton. "Enjoy your rewards in *Valhalla* until you are called to *Ragnarök.*" Finally, Freyja covered the area with more stones. There would be no way, after

several more nights of fierce wind, that any evidence of a
burial would be visible.

CHAPTER FOURTEEN

Freyja sat with her back against the boulder facing the rising sun. She was not sure how she had gotten there. She looked down to see her apron dress was covered with dirt and noted the dried streak of blood down her right arm. Both filthy arms ached but her wounds were shallow and did not hurt greatly. She grimaced as she tried to reposition herself more comfortably. She knew it would grow hot soon so she began to crawl on her hands and knees wearily to the other side of the boulder and the shade. Something hard was clutched in and hanging from her hand. She sat back on her haunches and opened her hand. The necklace had imprinted itself upon the skin of her palm. Bright gold and amber glittered in a bed of dust.

She pulled one side from the ring clasp and started to raise it to her neck. Something made her stop and she shook her foggy head. When she realized what she had almost done, she began to tremble fearing the fate that might have manifested had she worn it. It was not her necklace and could never belong to her. It would be an offering to the goddess. Part of the blot to *Freyja* and *Freyr*.

She reached for her belt pouch and pried the gritty strings open. The necklace joined a few dirty pieces of dried rabbit.

Continuing to crawl, she discovered a substantial pooling of water under the rock. Her mead skin had been left there so she lay on her belly and eagerly filled it. Freyja drank all that she could hold, gasping between mouthfuls. It was slow going because the space beneath the boulder was shallow, but she was more than grateful for the water. She sat cross legged and pulled the bottom of her underdress to the water to use as a rag for her face. Though not sure she had accomplished much, it felt good and she settled into the shade to sleep.

Freyja woke to the shriek of a sea eagle and the sun in her eyes. The great bird was diving near several large boulders repeatedly and then returning to the one tree she could see to the north. Its white tail caught the last of the sunlight. She stood and recognized that *Sol* was beginning her descent behind the trees on the horizon. Her eyes widened with the thought that the eagle might have lost a prey and thus she might gain a *nattmal* meal. She stood and lifted her stiff skirts to walk toward the boulders. She shook out the fabric and created a cloud of dust to follow her. She opened her mouth and laughed loudly at the thought of the sight she was making. Her mouth filled with dust and she had to stop to cough and spit out the grit.

The laughter drove the sea eagle again to the top of the lone tree. It seemed to eye her as she approached, sliding now and then on a loose thin rock. When she got next to the boulders, she heard the snuffling of a pig. She leaned over to peer between the rocks and saw a small boar. It was clearly alive though it had claw marks from the talons of the bird. She stood up and waved her arms to scare away the bird. When it did not move, she began to throw rocks at it. They did not reach the top of the tree, but seemed to make the bird give up. It shrieked loudly as it circled overhead, then flew off toward the setting sun.

She lay on her side and reached an arm in to touch the pig. She grabbed a leg and pulled. The pig did not want to come out so she tried again. This time she got ahold of both back legs and pulled. The pig just fit through the opening. It seemed to pop out and she sat down hard with a small pig in her lap. She began to giggle, rocking the pig in her arms like a baby. She would have no food, but by some miracle had found a boar for *Freyr*. "Hail, the gods," she yelled to the sky. Perhaps one had sent the eagle. "Thank you, eagle and thank you land *vaettir*."

Freyja looked down into her lap and saw that the pig had made itself comfortable and was munching happily on something. It was a mushroom! She laughed with delight. A boar and edible mushrooms. She quickly went to her belly and felt through the opening in the rocks again. She pulled out a handful of mushrooms and laid them on the ground beside her. Again and again, she pulled out handfuls and knew she would have a large pile. She rolled over to sit up and saw that the little boar was helping himself to the mushrooms. She shook her head and smiled. She would happily share with him as he was her good fortune.

The mushrooms bulged her pouch as she filled it and she picked up the pig in her arms. As the sun slowly set, they picked their way over rocks back to her boulder. She started a fire and the little pig joined her in eating more of the mushrooms. A piece of dried rabbit went well with the mushrooms after it was rinsed off. Freyja sighed. Her task was almost complete. In the morning she would begin the climb down the hill with a necklace and a small boar. She would be sure to make an offering to the land *vaettir* in thanks and wondered if it would be enough to counteract Karle's disrespect.

Freyja stood to place some mushrooms and a bite of rabbit on top of the boulder. "Hail, the land *vaettir*. I thank you for your help on my journey and honor you for your keeping of this place. I will leave you in peace in the morning. Hail, the land *vaettir*." Freyja sat with a deep sigh and then laid down near the fire. The wind picked up and began its howling. She closed her eyes as the little pig settled next to her sharing warmth. She slept deeply and did not dream.

She was in the shade when she woke so added the last of the wood pile to the fire. She gave the pig some mushrooms then put water in her palm. It sucked a bit of it off her hand. After enjoying the warmth of the fire for a bit Freyja stirred the coals and kicked some dirt on it. As she kicked, she noticed the *seax* that she had received from the shield-maiden wight. She had forgotten about it, but now tucked it at her waist. It felt cold and she reacted with a slight shiver.

"Thank you shield-maiden. Thank you, *Grjot Fell.* Thank you land *vaettir* and Hail the gods. We ask for safe journey down the mountain side," Freyja yelled as loudly as she could into the crisp morning air. She picked up the little pig and began her back-and-forth pattern of walking, down the hill. The sun rose and sweat dripped into her eyes. The pig was not that heavy, but a burden, nonetheless. She stopped every so often to wipe her brow with her cloak and rest her arms.

By midday the sun was high and she had to walk over new ground instead of the way she had walked up the hill. Karle's rockslide had changed the pathways and many were now unstable. She put out a foot carefully for each step and many times rocks fell out from beneath her foot. Testing each step took time, but they were nearing the tree where she and Karle had camped. There was little shade under the tree just now, but she was anxious to get to the promised shade. Freyja plodded on, with her jaw set, knowing that she could soon rest.

Finally reaching the tree and its shade, Freyja sank down on a rock and put the pig down. Her mead skin still held some water so she drank a bit and gave some to the pig. There was only a little wood left. Karle must have used up their pile. She looked, but could find no food left behind. There were some blood stains on a rock near the fire and the rope that had held the goat. That could now be used for the pig. "A small thing, but thank you Karle," Freyja mumbled.

She and the pig ate a few mushrooms and she began to search for sticks for the fire. She planned for tonight only, then would continue down the hill in hopes of making it to the waterfall. She pinched the skin on the back of her hand and it stayed raised for a bit. This showed that her body was in great need of water. Tomorrow, with the gods help, she would have water. The search for wood took her in a widening circle and when she returned to the shade, she felt dizzy. She lay down and closed her eyes to wait for it to pass. Slowly she sat up and built the fire at sunset. The wind rose again, as its pattern had been every night, and she sat against the tree with the little pig. Her face felt dull and she let herself sink into rest. Darkness enveloped her bringing relief to her dry eyes. She pulled out the mead skin and lifted it to her lips. She was able to suck out only a small mouthful and for that she was grateful. "Hail, the gods. I hope you find favor with my journey and lead me quickly to water."

Just before dawn, Freyja awakened to a light rain. The pig had found a small indentation in the dirt and sat in it, anticipating a wallow. Freyja lifted her face and let the drops run down her front with a smile of relief. A bit of water pooled on top of a rock and she wet the bottom of her underdress. She sucked as much water as she could out of the cloth and did it again and again. The pig snuffled happily as it drank and wallowed. The rain was short-lived and soon the sun rose over *Grjot Fell*. Freyja tied the rope around the pig's neck and kicked out the last of the steaming coals of the fire.

As much as she had welcomed the rain, the moisture now made walking hazardous. The flat rocks were slick with a coating of mud. Freyja held out her arms wide for balance as she led the pig on the rope during her back-and-forth journey. She smiled wryly as she thought of the *Valkyries* looking down to see this silly sight. A woman dressed in dirt stiffened clothing leading a muddy pig down the rocky peak. She must look as lonely and half crazed as she felt. Only those not of *Midgard* would see her now and they could make what they would of her.

Freyja picked a tree on the edge of the underbrush and made that her goal. She believed that it was where she had gathered berries. The thought of the juicy little fruits made her mouth water. It would be a good place to rest. Intent on that goal, she continued at a slow and steady pace.

When she reached the tree, she reached out a hand to touch the bark. She couldn't quite believe it was real. She steadied herself touching the rough bark beneath her palm and she smelled the scent of the moist undergrowth. Pushing between some bushes she entered a clearing that was surrounded by berries. Freyja went to her knees and began picking and popping the sweet jewels into her mouth. The pig eagerly nuzzled her juice-stained hand. She laughed and gave berries to the little boar who squealed with delight.

Freyja started to gag and fought with all her might not to vomit. She laid down on her side, curling up and drawing her knees up. Her stomach felt full for the first time in many days. She breathed slowly to let her body welcome the nourishment and her belly settle down. After a long while she heard a man's voice yelling, "Get back here. You have what I need." She sat up slowly. The sound was near the waterfall so she and the boar started walking in that direction.

When they could hear the waterfall, the pig seemed to get excited. It pulled on the rope toward the smell of water. Freyja followed, licking her lips. They walked around a large tree and came to the pool below the waterfall. Freyja laid on her belly, lips to water and started to drink. She caught herself and sat back on her haunches, busily washing her face and arms. A muddy pool collected below her knees.

"You are here," Karle yelled. Freyja turned to look at him. He had made a crutch from a branch and was standing near a wood pile by a fire pit. He held a leafy branch in the other hand and must have been offering it to the goat. The goat! Here it was, with Karle. It wandered up to Freyja and bleated at her. Freyja reached down to scratch its head.

Freyja turned her back on Karle and sat again at the edge of the pool. She took off her boots and thrust her feet into the cool water. Karle hobbled over to her. "I see you have a boar. It is quite small. Will it be worthy? I have been waiting for you. I have fire and goat's milk to offer you as a good host."

"Thank you," said Freyja. "I will accept your hospitality after I bathe. I go to the waterfall. Do not follow." She glared at Karle and pulled the pig after her as they went through the brush. The goat began to follow them.

"Come back you stupid goat. I must milk you," Karle whined after them.

Freyja put the pig's rope down near the waterfall and rested a rock on the end. He could get in the water to drink and bathe along with her. She carefully laid down her belt, pouch, knife, and *seax*. She then put her apron dress on top of them, followed by her cloak. She wore her underdress into the waterfall and began to rub the dirt out of it. She took it off and used it as a rag to scrub her body and then beat it on some rocks and rinsed it clean. The wound on her arms had closed and she washed off the crusted blood. Her skinned knee had a good, though dirty scab which also cleaned up a bit. She felt lighter as each layer of dirt was shed from her body. Sandy dirt fell from her hair as she rinsed it again and again.

Stepping out of the falls, Freyja spread her underdress on some bushes to dry while she took her apron dress into the water. The dirt had so encrusted the fabric that she might need to boil it clean. She pounded out of it what she could and took it to the bushes. She did the same for her cloak. Putting on the underdress she let it finish drying on her body as she looked through her things. Everything got a rinsing off in the water. She soaked her pouch and rubbed it between her fingers. She opened it and let water run through it, but did not want any of this world to see the necklace yet. She picked up her belongings and the rope to the pig and walked barefooted back to the pool.

There she spread out her overdress and cloak to continue drying on a bush. Her other things lay directly under them. She called the goat over to Karle by the fire. "Here, I will hold her while you milk." She saw that he had the bowl ready. He stared at her for a bit and then began to milk the goat. He kept glancing at her in her underdress. Freyja pursed her mouth in disgust.

The bowl full of milk, Karle lifted it to his lips and noisily began to drink. Half of the bowl went quickly, then he looked at Freyja and held the bowl out to her. "Have what you will. The goat eats happily and will make more." He smiled.

Freyja nodded and took the bowl. It tasted heavenly, but she drank slowly and only a little. She pointedly took the bowl to the offering rock and poured some out for the land *vaettir*, whispering her thanks. Then she handed the empty bowl back to Karle and placed her boots under a tree near the fire. The ground there did not look disturbed. Karle must sleep in another spot. She pulled off some spruce branches to make a sleeping pallet for herself then checked her cloak and apron dress. The apron dress was dry so she began to put it over her underdress.

"You may dress as you like here, Freyja. No one comes, but us," Karle leered at her.

"Just so, Karle. You are here," Freyja said. She continued to dress and added her belt with pouch and knife. The *seax* remained under her cloak. She was no longer hot, no longer dirty, and no longer starving, but she was still tired. "I will rest now. You must leave me alone," she said adjusting her belt.

"I will take the goat's rope back. It will be easier for my foot," Karle pointed to his swollen ankle.

"If you make a pen for the pig, you may take back the rope. You lost the rope because of your own doing," Freyja remarked dryly. She lay back and closed her eyes. She heard Karle grumbling as she dozed.

She woke from her rest with someone kissing her feet. Was that right? No kissing her neck. She looked down at her feet and the little pig was there. It was wet. But her neck? Karle had curled around her from behind and was lightly kissing her neck. "We have worked hard on this journey and should know passion as our reward," Karle spoke softly and placed his hand on her hip. Freyja turned slowly towards him and then kicked his sore ankle. He howled, "You are a troll. Daughter of a whore."

"And you?" Freyja had sprung up and leaned over him, her knife drawn. "You have done nothing to help our journey. You have not worked hard and the gods know that you lie. You have broken a sworn oath." Freyja was starting to cry with her rage. "I start back now," she said while wiping her tears with the back of her hand.

"But it will be dark soon," Karle whimpered.

Freyja went to fill her water skin and the mead skin from the pool. She put on her cloak, putting the *seax* under the back of her belt then picked up the pig. She stalked forward on the path back to the west-leading road. Karle grabbed the rope he had tied to the goat. He put on his cloak, and using his crutch, began to follow. "I am coming, Freyja," he said tremulously.

"The sun sets now, Freyja. May we stop and build a fire? I fear the Wild Hunt," Karle yelled, sometime later, from behind the girl. "I see much wood for a fire."

"Karle, you know it is not the time for the Wild Hunt," Freyja replied over her shoulder. She kept on walking.

"But the other night, I saw the lights," Karle said. "We should stop to be safe."

"The other night was something else. Perhaps *Valkyries* tending to the fallen," Freyja smiled as she fingered the pouch at her waist. She stopped to turn around and noticed that Karle was not keeping pace with her. His foot was slowing him down. Taking pity on him she chose a spot off the path where others had camped before. "I will start the fire and you can milk the goat when you get here," Freyja shook her head. She started a good fire with much wood piled nearby. She spread out her cloak on some long grasses to make her bed and sat down cross-legged.

Freyja had opened her pouch and was looking inside when Karle arrived. "I will milk the goat. What do you have there?" he asked. "Any food?"

Freyja tied the strings of the pouch and put it back on her belt. "I do have some mushrooms and one piece of dried rabbit meat," she remarked. She went back into the pouch and pulled out the mushrooms and the rabbit.

"Oh, I saw something shining from your pouch. Did you find the amber?" Karle quizzed her with wide eyes.

"Ah, yes. I found amber and this boar for the offering to *Freyja* and *Freyr*." Freyja quickly shut the pouch again. She placed the rabbit meat on a rock and pounded it with another rock to break it in two. She put one piece and a handful of mushrooms on top of a rock on the far side of the fire. The pig came over to investigate, but Freyja enticed him with more mushrooms back to her cloak. "We will be back at your farm by midday. I know they will be happy to see you."

"They will not be happy when they see my foot." Karle made a sour face." They only look to me as labor for the farm."

"But one day, you will inherit the farm," Freyja said encouragingly.

"I hope to prove myself at raiding. Perhaps I can have others on the farm. Maybe a wife?" Karle looked pointedly at Freyja.

"Karle, you must stop this want of me. I am for Sven as everyone knows. When he is back you will see. Besides, there are other girls who look at you," Freyja giggled.

Karle had filled the bowl with goat's milk and deftly plucked out a goat's hair. He raised it to his lips and drank half then handed the bowl to Freyja. "Perhaps you will learn to share with a woman first. They like that," said Freya. She took the bowl and poured some milk into her hand for the pig, then she put some on a stone for the land *vaettir* and thanked them. Finally, she drank every last drop of the delicious milk. She handed back the bowl and shared mushrooms with the pig as she quietly gnawed at the rabbit meat. She was beginning to feel herself again with food and water.

Karle sat by the rock where Freyja had left the food. He ate at the rabbit meat slowly, then he looked down at his ankle. "I do not know how to tell of this." He pointed at his foot.

"Tell everyone a good story, but know that I know what is true," said Freyja slowly. "Perhaps you might tell them what you learned about how to make offerings to the land spirits?" she smiled. "It is truly a good story that you survived the rock slide." The goat came up to Karle. "Also, there is a story in the return of the goat. The land *vaettir* may have forgiven you, or perhaps a god has favored you?"

"And so it is!" Karle yelled with excitement. "*Thor's* cart is pulled by his goats. Surely he has favored me by returning my goat." That started Karle to making up stories about their adventure and his part in it. Freyja went to sleep as he jabbered on to the goat and the pig.

At the first light of morning Freyja heard Karle rustling about. He was drinking from his waterskin then he took his bowl to fill with berries. "Freyja," he called when he saw her sitting up. "I have berries for us, but first I offer some to the land *vaettir*." He made a big show of leaving some on the offering stone. Freyja smiled while shaking her head and held out a hand. Karle promptly filled it with berries. She watched Karle milk the goat and then watched him take some to the stone. "Now you may have some, Freyja. Always first to the *vaettir*," Karle said solemnly. He handed her the bowl and she made sure to only drink half of the milk and then handed it back to him.

The two began walking with their animals. Karle led the goat on a rope and Freyja was driving the pig with a switch. They moved slowly for Karle's foot still bothered him and they did not feel the need to hurry. At the meeting of the three roads, they saw several people cleaning up from some trading. Soon everyone would know that they had traveled back this morning, even if they had no idea of their leaving. When they got to the edge of Karle's family farm, a farm hand ran up to take the goat from Karle. A young girl ran to the house and Karle's mother soon scurried toward them.

"Oh, Karle. You have hurt yourself. Sit and rest," his mother said. She took his crutch and helped him lower down on a stump. Holding her grown son's weight against her growing belly looked uncomfortable, but she persisted. She nodded at Freyja while she examined the ankle. "You have seen this?" she asked Freyja. Her eyes narrowed while she scowled.

"Not really," replied Freyja. "We were not together for all of our journey."

"You mean, our *saga*!" Karle smiled broadly. He launched in on colorful descriptions of everything they had seen. His mother nodded while sending servants scurrying this way and that. They returned and she began dressing his ankle with a poultice. Karle barely noticed as he gestured wildly and exclaimed loudly. Several of the young servant girls stared at him, rapt with attention. His face was animated and happier than Freyja had seen him in a long time. He was the center of attention and Freyja took the opportunity

145

to leave, saying her thanks to his mother for the provisions she had sent.

Freyja knew that she must next visit the Old One to tell her of her journey. She had indeed done as the Old One instructed by taking "what things you need and also... a man that you may not need."

CHAPTER FIFTEEN

Freyja wanted terribly to see her home and to soak in the tub. She had lost track of the days, but she would bathe whatever day it was. She had a duty to report to the Old One first and so she walked off the path into the forest, the quickest way she knew. The pig was easy to drive with a switch and they ambled slowly to the farm. There was smoke coming from the hole in the roof of the hut and the skin was held open. Freyja bent down to grab the pig and entered the hut. "I have been waiting for you," the Old One nodded knowingly. She pointed to a place for Freyja to sit by the fire.

"Did you dream, or did the gods tell you I was coming?" asked Freyja in awe.

"No, the children have told me that you and Karle were seen walking with a goat and a boar. This is it?" She eyed the little pig critically. "Yes, it is good. We will fatten it well." She threw a handful of powder on the fire and orange smoke rose up and out the hole. A child came to the door soon after.

"Yes, *Amma?*"

"Take this pig to a pen and care for it well. It needs water and food right away." The Old One smiled at the child and waved her hand like the sweeping of a broom. Freyja offered the switch to the child and the child ran off with it and the pig.

"He was a good comfort on cold nights. A friend," mused Freyja thoughtfully.

"Cattle die and kinsmen die…" the Old One chuckled. "Now, of the amber, show me," demanded the woman. Freyja reached for the pouch at her belt and untied the string. She pulled out the necklace of gold and amber and the Old One's eyes went wide. She sucked in a large breath of air. "How did you come by this?" she asked Freyja with narrowed her eyes.

Freyja told the story of traveling to the waterfall pool and then the climb up *Grjot Fell*. She told of the rock slide and how Karle had gone back down the mountain and she traveled alone to the top, not knowing his fate. "I found a skeleton in the dark when I was searching for wood so came back with a torch. With the light I saw the necklace. I put the torch in the rocks and reached for the necklace. At my touch the wight gained flesh to become a shield-maiden." The Old One sniffed loudly and spat into the fire. Freyja continued with the tale of that night and showed the Old One the scar on her arm from the fight and lastly the *seax* that had also been given her in trade. "I gave her the honorable death she deserved and watched the *Valkyrie* carry her to *Valhalla*. I buried her with her sword as I promised. This is how I have come by the necklace and *seax* in trade."

"This is a powerful adventure you have had, Freyja. A most worthy gift for the Lady. Your reputation will grow when people know of this," the Old One rocked pursing her lips.

"I am forbidden to say how I got the necklace and *seax*. The shield-maiden does not want her family to know of her shame. How she came to be on *Grjot Fell* without her comrades," said Freyja quickly.

"We will say only that you have brought it to the goddess. And Karle had no part?" asked the old woman.

"Karle has not seen the necklace. He knows of amber that I found near the waterfall," replied Freyja.

"I will have my family carve a god post for The Lady, *Freyja*. They will bury the *seax* at the base," spoke the Old One. The Old One nodded thoughtfully then shook her head. "And what of the boar? How was it found?"

"It was gifted by the gods." Freyja laughed and told how a sea eagle must have dropped the pig between the rocks and its cries alerted Freyja. "I came to see what prey I might have for a meal, but found the boar. The next day we walked back to our fire pit where I found blood from Karle's foot and the goat's rope he had left. On the following day we got back to the pool to find Karle and the goat waiting."

"I have not offered you food nor drink, Freyja. I will make us tea while you eat of this cheese and hazelnuts." She pushed a bowl toward Freyja who had to make herself slow down to not gobble it up. "I am sure that Karle's mother is doting on him. He will be well fed and cared for." She had a distasteful look on her face.

"When I left him, his mother was tending to his ankle. She glared at me as if I should have nursed him. I did not give them time to offer me food nor drink," Freyja giggled. "I had no desire to stay."

"As the runes said, Karle was certainly a man that you may not need," tittered the Old One. Both women chuckled at that.

The Old One poured tea for them both and they sat quietly for a bit. "Now to your farm. Your mother has been thinking of you." They stood up together and the Old One embraced Freyja. "You have done well. We will offer your gifts at the harvest blot."

Chapter Sixteen

Several moon cycles passed and it was time for first harvest. The grain was tall and herbs were being hung to dry. Berries bunched ripe on the vines and the first crab apples were getting ready to fall. Mouths watered for items that would soon be available for trade as well. The harvest had come for them. At the Mead House, and during market day trading, farmers compared the readiness of their barley and made plans for when the harvest festival should be held.

Soon the call went out and the first sheaf of grain on each farm was harvested and bound for *Odin* and the land *vaettir* in thanks. A few more were cut so that wives could make the first loaves of bread to take to *Freyfest*. Everyone would take the best of their harvest to the farm of the Old One to celebrate the Lord, *Freyr*. Arndis and Freyja gathered a bounty of radishes, sorrel, and berries along with eggs and several rabbits for the pots. As they walked the path, they heard the voices of others ahead. They were joined by the twins' farm family, their cart loaded with barley ale and mead. Everyone was well-dressed and in a festive mood, as in every year.

The farm had trestles set up outside and the boards were being set with all the plenty brought from the local farms. Laughter and singing filled the air and most faces held smiles. Fires dotted the area with pots hanging over, and the smell of bread frying made everyone inhale more deeply.

At midday, the Old One appeared in her best clothes. She lit a torch from a fire and held it high. "In *Thor's* name we light this flame to banish all baleful wights and wills from this place. We cleanse this place and make it holy." She handed the torch to her son who walked a circle around the gathering. When he returned, she picked up a hammer. She raised it to each of the four directions and spoke, "*Thor Vigi.*" "*Thor* blesses," was repeated by all as she made the hammer sign.

The Old One approached the altar. It had been decorated with barley, honeycombs, crab apples, berries, and various bounty from the farms and forest. The smooth slightly slanted stone seemed ready to accept the sacrifice. The godpost for *Freyr* had been cleaned and looked down on the stone altar.

Freyr's godpost had been on the Old One's farm as long as Freyja could remember. It was made from a spruce tree as big around as a man. The bark had been peeled from it and the face of the god had been carved near the top. His large eyes seemed to look down on the people kindly and his smile, surrounded by his beard, was wide and warm.

Next to it another godpost had been erected. "What is this?" whispered Arndis to Freyja. Her eyes were questioning.

"You shall see," Freyja answered her, in a whisper also. She put her finger to her lips.

A godpost for *Freyr's* twin sister, *Freyja*, was newly carved of a pine tree. The bark had been peeled to reveal a trunk which appeared to be golden. Smaller around, but just as tall, it stood to the side of *Freyr's* post and the sacrifice stone. The goddess' eyes were wide and she wore a small smile. Her braided hair had been carved to reach halfway down the length of the tree. Sap had welled up and run down her face from her eyes. At its base was earth newly disturbed piled around. Freyja noticed that in front there was a low mound, the length of an arm. She caught the Old One's eye and looked pointedly at the earth where she assumed the *seax* had been buried. The Old One nodded and they both smiled, acknowledging the safety of the shield-maiden's secret.

The Old One raised her voice. "At this time of first fruits of the harvest we honor the god *Freyr*. To the Lord we give thanks for bringing life to our fields." There was an appreciative murmur from the crowd. "We also give thanks to *Thor* as god of the harvest and his wife, *Sif*, with golden hair that we see in our ripe grain." Again, another murmur. "*Freyr* gave much to win the hand of his love, *Gerd*. As he sacrificed, we sacrifice to him today." The fattened pig was brought to the altar and a roar went up from the crowd.

"The boar comes to *Freyr* from our own Freyja, who must also work for the abundance of our people. To ensure the prophecy for our village the gods tasked her with bringing a boar from *Grjot Fell* to this *Freyrsblot*." Many heads bobbed in appreciation. "She was also asked to find a gift of amber for the goddess *Freyja* from the rocky peak. This is why we honor the Lady with her own godpost." Freyja raised her eyebrows at her mother. "What better way to ensure fertility and prosperity for our village than to ask for the help of the twin children of *Njord*?"

Two young men lifted the boar on to the altar and held it in place. Freyja came to the pig and stroked it with her hand. "Hail the gods. I thank you for bringing this boar to me as a symbol of plenty. I thank the pig for giving its life to honor *Freyr* at this autumn sacrifice." She lowered her voice to a whisper. "I thank the pig for its gift of being a friend, during my quest, when I had no other."

The Old One handed Freyja her ceremonial knife. Freyja blinked away tears as she reached forward to slit the pig's throat. As the blood poured down the altar several people rushed forward to catch it in bowls while the people cheered. With her hands still wet with blood, Freyja reached into the pouch at her waist and brought out the pieces of amber she had found near the waterfall. She held them high for all to see then placed them at the base of the *Freyja* godpost. Another cheer from the people filled the air. The people knew nothing of the necklace and the trade that Freyja had made for it. Freyja and the Old One had kept the shield-maiden's secret.

A woman handed the Old One a bowl filled with blood and she turned to the crowd. All gathered close to face her as she dipped a spruce branch into the blood. With a large movement she raised it high above her and brought it down forcefully. Again, she dipped the branch into the blood and raised it high to the side to fling it sideways. The people cheered both times as they were anointed with the blood of the sacrifice to the gods. The Old One took what blood was left in the bowl to stand between the two godposts. "From the gods, to the earth, to us," she spoke seriously. "From us, to the earth, to the gods," she said as she poured out the blood upon the earth.

The boar was then carried away to the cook pots and horns and cups appeared, ready to be filled. Several women came forward with barley ale to fill them.

The Old One watched and when all had some ale, she held her horn high and yelled toward the sky, as loudly as she could, "Hail the gods!" All drank. "Hail to Lord *Freyr, Thor,* and *Sif* for the fertility and abundance of the land." All drank again. "Hail to the Lady, *Freyja* for passion and prosperity. The unveiling of our prophecy." As they raised their drinking vessels their eyes were drawn to the top of the *Freyja* godpost. There, around the neck of the carved goddess, shimmered a golden necklace, catching the rays of the afternoon sun. It was hard to see in the bright sunlight and many may have just thought it was a trick of the light.

Now the cooking was in earnest and the drinking as well. "Eh, Freyja. Well done on your gifts for the gods. Now you will fulfill the prophecy. When Sven and the others get home, we will get to the hard work of the harvest and you two will get working hard too!" said an old farmer as he walked past and smacked her on the behind.

Karle came up to Freyja with several girls trailing him. They were giggling at every word he said. One even carried his drinking horn. "Freyja, I am telling them the tale of our adventure." He was not leaning on his crutch very much, except when he needed it for show.

"Oh, here let me help you sit," said one brunette. "I'll take your crutch," said another. "Let me go fill your drinking horn," said a strawberry blonde beauty. Karle looked at Freyja and shrugged with a broad smile.

Freyja found her mother at a fire, busy with cooking. "Ah, Freyja we have a good porridge cooking. Will you stir while I check the bread?" Arndis asked. She did not wait for a reply, but thrust Freyja toward the pot. A woman came by with ale for the cooks so Freyja helped herself as well. She could see several kettles of porridge that seemed a mix of many good things. Bread was being fried in pans thrust in and out of the fires and the boar was being boiled in several of the very large kettles further down the way. The smells made a heavenly mix and Freyja's stomach rumbled loudly.

One of the cooks nodded in sympathy and picked up a disk of bread that she then broke into many pieces. She passed the pieces out to the cooks on duty who took a minute to enjoy the bread with their ale. Arndis even took a piece and a moment. When the cooking was done the women started to plate the food and take it to the boards.

Hungry hands reached for helpings, but all was shared as all had brought, each from their own farm. As the eating slowed the voices quieted a bit. The people were feeling the abundance of early harvest and the blessings of the gods. The sunlight began to fade and torches were lit in places away from the fires. Some were making places for their children to sleep and others were packing up to leave.

Arndis saw the twins' family packing their cart. "Do you leave? If so, may we ride with you?" she asked the tall father. There seemed much room in the cart, now offloaded.

He nodded yes and Arndis and Freyja sat at the back of the cart with their legs hanging over. The jostling kept them awake along with the loud snoring of the mother who had eaten and drunk well this night.

When their trail led off from the path, Arndis and Freyja said their goodnights in hushed voices and watched the cart rumble away.

When they reached their steps, they got to their beds quickly, filled with good food and drink.

Chapter Seventeen

Weeks passed, cooling temperatures heralding the fall, and animals were getting ready for winter. Arndis was working in the garden and Freyja was taking dried rabbit pelts down from the wall when they heard the horn sound. "Oh, *Odin*, it must be them," she whispered in hope. Freyja dropped her pelts and ran to the rocky prominence from where she could see. "They are very near," she screamed to her mother. "If I ride hard, I can meet them as they land," she breathlessly giggled.

"Well, off then. I will meet you at the Mead House to hear the tales and celebrate," Arndis stood to brush the dirt off her skirts. "I hope you will bring your man back with you to our house where he now belongs," she added with a great smile. As she watched Freyja on the old stallion start down the path to the side of *fjord*, she remembered taking the journey herself. She had never had a lover to meet this way and had a moment's thought of regret for a life other than her own.

Arndis shook the old dreams from her mind, then hurried into the house. She thought of the love that her parents had always shown to each other. Their life had been as hard as many, but they always had smiles for one another. She was reminded further of her parent's love as she brought a skin from their bed to add to Freyja's for the extra body expected. She could almost hear her mother speak. *If only you had had such fortune, as I, my sweet daughter.* She hummed as she swept and tidied the farm house. Then she grabbed her shawl and Freyja's new shawl for the anticipated cool walk home that night. She sang all the way to the Mead House.

As the village ship sighted their shores, Sven swiftly let out his breath in one long sigh of relief. He had successfully experienced his first viking. Fought, raided, hunted, and returned. Now he wanted the quiet farming life, at least until next viking. He glimpsed Freyja riding along the beach and readied himself nervously. He knew he had a duty to be with her, but the fire that she had kindled within his belly had been slowly dying over these months. Still, he could not help feeling excited watching her breasts move and her well-muscled thighs grip her horse tightly as she rode. For a moment he mused about *"inn matki munr,"* but the captain approached with a loud voice, shaking him free from his thoughts.

"You now have a new responsibility to the village," the captain shouted above the raucous breaking waves. "You will guard our captive, the Far Isle chief's daughter. No harm will befall her, no man will lay hands upon her. Also, you... *You* would not want to touch things you should not touch," the captain directed a stern look at Sven. "You will swear to this?"

Sven sighed deeply, wanting only his farm life. "Yes, Gunnar, I swear."

"The village prophecy and prosperity depend upon you. After all, 'When Freyja and Sven couple and children are born then we will trade with many and our village will prosper.' Who is to say that ransom is not also trade?" chuckled Gunnar.

Sven nodded to the captain, watching others jump overboard to beach the ship. Warriors were besieged by their families and passed their treasure into waiting hands. Women wrapped their arms around husbands and sons to welcome them home. Children clambered onto their fathers and were then put quickly to work. Many began their journey home with calls of farewell. Those not going home were heading toward the Mead House to celebrate their return and share stories.

Sven watched them all leave toward the village and focused on gathering his belongings. He thought he heard a shout on the wind and looked down the beach to see Freyja very close.

Freyja had caught short glimpses of the beach through the trees lining the path. The boat had appeared low in the water as it approached the shore. She could see now that the boat was overfilled with bundles and barrels from her vantage point on the side of the *fjord*. This was a good sign as it meant a prosperous viking. She caught a breath and bit her lip as she searched for Sven's golden head above the rest. Many of the heads were of golden hair, but his should be taller than most and she was sure she would know it. There were two figures in dark hoods that she could not place. They were not bound as slaves so she was sure to find out more about them. That could wait, it was of no concern to her now. A smile of good nature spread across her face and anticipation rose in her belly at the thought of being with him again. Her thighs were becoming warm from contact with the back of the stallion and her groin sensitive as she imagined Sven against her. She could not wait to smell his warm musk fragrance, to feel his well-muscled chest meet hers. She longed to wake and look into his eyes each morning and remember with joy, the words of love spoken the night before. She could almost taste the sweetness of their greeting kiss which would begin this new time together.

She was dying to get to the boat and close to Sven by the time she had descended the hillside and was on the beach. The horse was slowing, his hooves now dealing with the dry sand. She felt her impatience grow as she urged the horse with her heels. The boat was beached and she was not yet there. Her lips twisted in a frustrated pout. Villagers were helping unload and shouts of greeting reached her ears. Because of the wind none heard her shouts to them, but went about their business. She raised a hand when Sven looked her way, but he was pulled away by the captain who was pointing. Sven then quickly jumped over the side. He reached back up to help a cloaked figure over the side. He seemed to bow under the weight, but carried the person and put them down on shore. He returned to help the other and his movements were different. He seemed to cradle this person and stepped carefully to bring them ashore. They remained close like this, standing still for a long time, until Sven placed the figure down gently.

The two figures in dark cloaks and many others walked away from the ship. Soon only three men were left; thank the gods that Sven was among them. The other two men busied themselves with packing their bundles, but Sven seemed mesmerized, looking after the dark figures, with his back to her. Who were they and what interest did he have in them? Sven looked well and whole and safely returned to her so she thought of *Frigga's* blessing with a smile and said a quick thank you. When she was close enough to run the rest of the way, she jumped off the horse. Laughing and gasping, she ran with determination. A joyful giggle rose in her throat as she opened her arms to engulf him in surprise with a side hug, her arm wrapped around his waist.

Sven looked down to see a disheveled farm woman enfolding him. He smiled and nodded a greeting then pushed Freyja gently back. "I have much to gather. Will you help?" Freyja's eyes brightened and she pushed the hair back from her face.

"I will always help my man. I have waited long and can wait a few minutes more," she smiled playfully then patted Sven on the butt. Sven smiled awkwardly and looked toward the other men. Sven spread several large cloths on the ground and pointed to a pile of items. Freyja knelt to put items in the center of one of the cloths. There were two silver goblets, delicately carved combs, and spoons and chains of silver that she put into the center of the cloth. Freyja unpinned her apron overdress and pulled down her underdress. She put four long chains of silver around her neck and felt the cold of the metal against her skin. She touched Sven's arm so that he looked down at her. They both immediately noticed her nipples harden with the cold of the necklaces and the wind. Freyja stood and reached for Sven's hand to pull to her breasts. Sven stumbled forward to place one hand behind Freyja's back while his other reveled in the touch of her nipples under his hand. His lips brushed her neck while he twirled her nipples between his fingers. He then bent his head to bring his lips to her nipples and Freyja arched her back offering herself to him. She moaned as he suckled upon her.

Sven pulled them both upright and brought his mouth to hers. The kiss was as sweet and deep as Freyja had imagined. The warmth of their mouths together seemed to radiate down to her belly as they hungrily tasted the familiar sweetness that they had been without these past months.

In time, Freyja broke off from the kiss and pulled Sven by the hand toward a fallen tree. They both quickly glanced toward the men busy at the ship who were not paying attention to them at all. Sven followed Freyja's lead eagerly anticipating more from the beautiful woman guided by the goddess of sex and love. When they neared the log Freyja jumped upon Sven, wrapped her legs around him and knocked him to the sand behind the huge barrier that provided just the smallest bit of privacy. "Sven, you are for

Freyja," she sang as she enfolded him. A smile of delight lit his face as he lifted her with both arms to take in her visage. She was breathless and knew she must look windblown and flushed. Suddenly she blushed with this attention and wiggled loose.

Hands to each side of his head she lowered down to press her breasts into his face. She then moved to kiss him deliberately on the mouth. Laughing, she reached beneath his tunic to find his manhood. She stroked him enthusiastically and he quickly responded. His body was at her mercy, reacting as it was designed. She straddled him, and then urged him, with the weight of her own body, to roll over. As one who had been starved she devoured his love with wild ecstasy. She felt that she opened and took him inside of her soul as well as her body. As she had been guided to not wait for his love, she felt that she was taking it, conquering him with each thrust to which she willingly consented. This is what she had wanted and the prophecy demanded.

He, in kind, gave. He felt compelled to please her. He caressed her face and ran his hand down the side of her body to reacquaint himself with her form. Kneeling in the sand, he enfolded her within his arm to hold her close to his heart while he gave himself to her.

There on the beach they reclaimed the months lost to them in frenzied lust. Muscles and sinew undulating, together they performed a divine dance of love. Tears of joy, mixed with Freyja's playful laughter, were the only sounds during a quick passion play of breathless wordless devotion to their connection.

They lay side by side in their secluded place for some time, basking in togetherness. Sven whispered, "Freyja," over, and over again as he stroked her face and hair. Freyja hummed with pleasure at his touch and his long-awaited attention.

Their eyes locked and they both smiled sheepishly when they heard the voices of the men nearby, drawing them back to reality. Freyja sat up to quickly bring up her underdress and pin her apron dress. Sven stood, and then reached out a hand to help Freyja. Both breathless and laughing, they brushed the sand from each other. Looking down at the imprint they had left in the sand, they giggled shyly as they sought each other's hands. Gunnar had kept a polite distance, and now came over to them clapping Sven on the back. "My friend, you are properly welcomed home," Gunnar said with a wink to Freyja.

Sven's half smile and nod acknowledged the captain, but Freyja's smile was from ear to ear as she dropped Sven's hand to link her elbow with his, "Indeed, he is most happily welcomed."

"I hear that we have missed *Freyfest* and that it went well, thanks to Freyja," Gunnar said. Sven looked at Freyja with surprise and she beamed a smile at both men. "We are well in time to finish with bringing in the harvest as we do each year, all but Sven. You should know that Sven has sworn to a mission concerned with our voyage. Although you have surely missed him, he will be busy often so you must take advantage of what little time you will have together." Gunnar bade them goodbye to depart with the last voyager and they were left alone.

Freyja and Sven gathered the last of his spoils onto the cloths and tied up the bundles. Then they sat together on the same log that had sheltered them; Freyja's head nestled against the strong shoulder she had so dearly missed. She breathed in his scent and closed her eyes. Sven's eyes were focused in the direction of the path to the village, an odd expression on his face. She took his hand and entwined their fingers tightly. He let out a deep sigh.

Sven felt as if he had drunk too much mead. His thoughts were fuzzy. His body felt truly satisfied as his pent-up lust had been released with Freyja. He had been thinking so much of sex during this return journey and had given over his body to her artful maneuverings. Does one push away a horn full of mead just because he has not asked for it? His thoughts returned now to the ever present "prophecy" and Freyja's sexual wanting of him. He had given to Freyja what she had wanted at this greeting, but he knew she would want more of him in the future. The foretelling laid out a life together and children which meant he would be required to take Freyja on as a wife. (As he was not yet married, he could not simply make her a concubine.) His mind was spinning with all the details that were sure to come. Negotiations of bride price, and the morning gift from his family. Their living situation and then the responsibility of children. It all seemed so much. He wondered if he could please all the people in his village. He was no longer sure of his feelings of duty to fulfill the prophecy or Freyja's cravings.

Freyja could not guess what was in Sven's heart or mind, but she smiled. The future was theirs together. They had a predetermined fate in the life of the village. They must move forward and take their places. A couple would become as one and children would bring trade and prosperity. All would come to pass as had been foretold, but now there were bundles to load onto the horse. There were spoils to share, tales to hear, and love to make. Her heart was overflowing with love and gratitude. Sven was safely home and their future and the prophecy would surely now unfold.

OG'S HALL

VILLAGE

MEAD HOUSE

TWIN'S FAMILY

MEADOW

FARM OF
ARNDIS

SIGNAL FIRE

SPRING

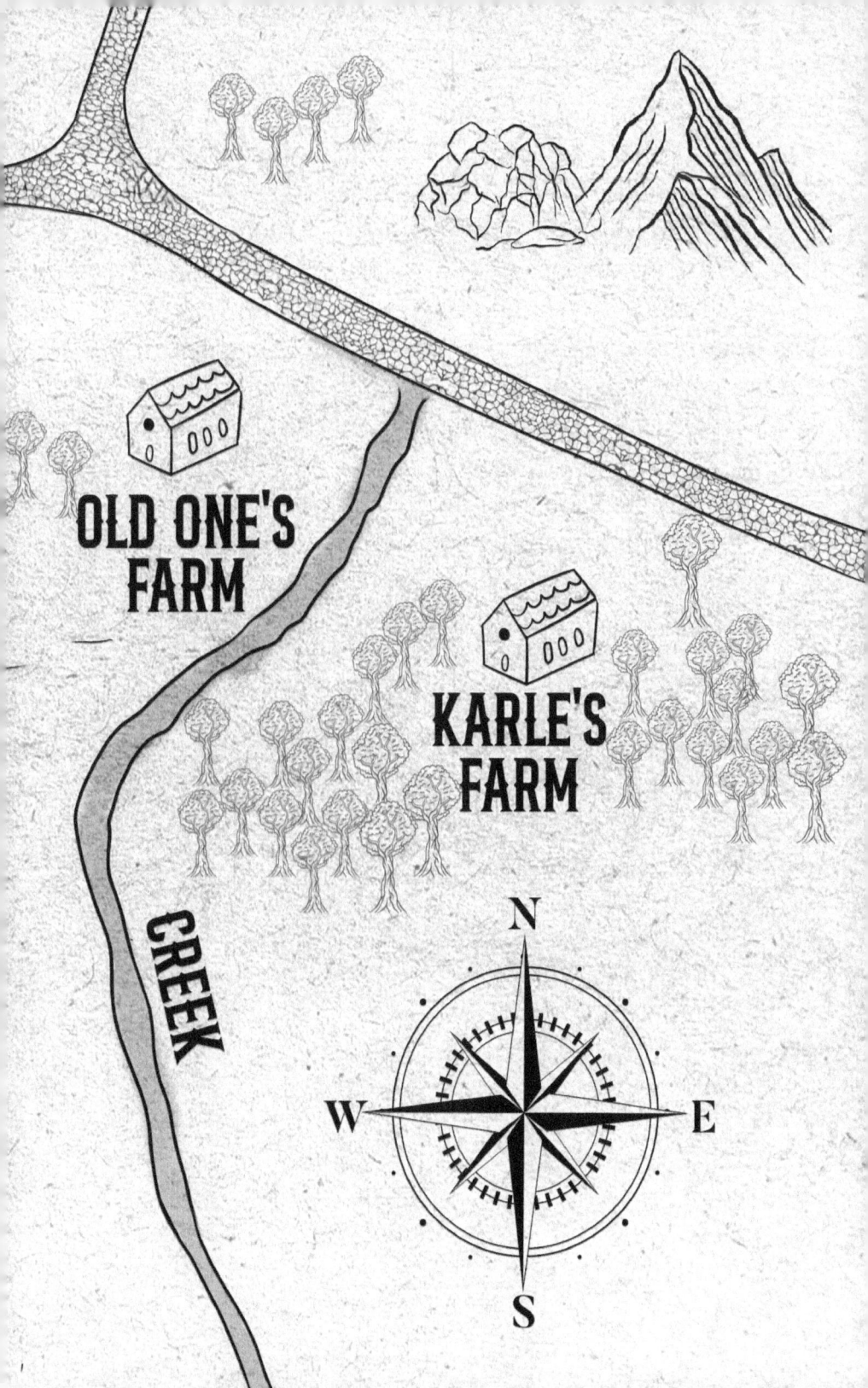

My Norse Prophecy fictional stories are inspired by Norse Pagan Gods/Goddesses and the traditions shared are those of the Viking Age. I have taken some license with variations of Germanic, Scandinavian, and Icelandic Pagan/Heathenism. My hope is that you will be encouraged to learn more for yourself through reading and research. My caution is that you be aware of groups and sources that may promote hate.

These stories are not intended to endorse White Supremacy, Supremacist or Nazi beliefs or practices. The travels of Viking Age Norse peoples took them around the world. They learned and borrowed from diverse cultures, especially through trade and intermarriage, thereby enriching their own culture. They sometimes settled in other parts of the world and brought their beliefs and culture to their adopted lands, as in the case of the Rus. Cultural diffusion was alive and well even in those early times.

"Odin is the All-Father,
not the Some Father!"